# The Last Great

# Halloween

A Trudy McFarlan
Novel
by

## Rootie Simms

Wilder Things Publishing
Orlando, Florida
wilderthingspublishing@hotmail.com

First Edition August 2015

The characters and events in this book are fictitious. The author used the names of places that are real, but the story within is fictitious. All characters described are a work of fiction, and have no relation to people living or dead. The only thing not fabricated is the family's love.

wilder things publishing

*This book is dedicated to everyone who keeps a
Sacred place in their heart for childhood Halloween.*


*And to Ken Eulo without whom this book could never have
been written. Thank you for your advice,
support, editing prowess, and love.
You are my champion.*


Note: The images on the back cover of this book are vintage Beistle
decorations from the 1960's. The Beistle Company has been producing
the best and spookiest art since 1923, making their images an indelible
part of childhood Halloween.

# THE LAST GREAT HALLOWEEN

# 1

Sometimes I do things I know are impossible but I do them anyway because there's always the teeniest, tiniest chance that they might be possible. And if a girl doesn't try, she'll never find out for sure.

This was one of those times.

I stood at the top of the driveway that led to my house. Our driveway is long and steep, covered with lumpy gravel that'll rip you to shreds if you slip and fall.

I took a deep breath. The air was cool and went into my lungs like peppermint.

I looked down the valley.

It was now officially fall because the leaves had turned orange, yellow, brown and red. Soon the leaves would fall off the trees and we'd rake them into piles for jumping. Then my dad would burn them, and my sisters, brother and I would dance around the fire like wild Indians—or, as my mother calls us—wild idiots.

But this was not the time to be thinking of fire-maddened Indians. This was a time to focus, because if I didn't do it soon, something would get away from me. I didn't know what it was that was getting away, but something surely was. I could just feel it.

There's something about autumn, when summer isn't quite over and winter isn't quite here that makes everything feel so temporary, so *urgent*. It's like, when I watch the leaves on the trees turn colors. I know the leaves are going to fall, and once they do they'll never get back on that tree again. So whatever those leaves have to do, whatever dreams they still have, they have to do it *now*—before they end up as a pile of flames with a bunch of wild idiots dancing around them.

I took one last look at the sky. It was dark purple and filled with evil-looking clouds that curled across the treetops—perfect for my experiment. A cold wind blew up the hill, ruffling my hooded sweatshirt, and I shivered. It was getting late. If I didn't do this soon, mom would stick her head out the door and yell at me to come home.

I gathered all my energy for this, my most glorious feat. Perhaps today the wild winds of autumn would bless my attempt.

Ready...set...*go!*

I ran down the treacherous driveway as fast as I could get my legs to pump. Faster and faster, my feet pounding against the gut-ripping gravel, the driveway nothing but a blur beneath my flashing feet. And coming on me fast—the stone stairway.

Dad had dug steps out of the bottom of the hill. Then he jammed flagstone into the dirt and made stairs out of the muddy hillside. I was now approaching the most dangerous part of my experiment.

But with danger comes a bridge across the impossible.

I reached the steps and, with crazy mad momentum, I jumped high in the air and soared down the stairs, my feet never touching the steps.

I remembered to concentrate on the feel of leathery wings unfurling from my shoulder blades, feel my teeth growing long and pointed. Because that's how you get the transformation to happen, through sheer concentration.

And for one glorious moment I was airborne, released from the gravitational pull of the earth. A thrill went through me, I was close to success…

Then my feet hit the ground and my legs buckled. I rolled head over heels, tumbling in the cold autumn grass.

In the excitement of near success I hadn't noticed my nine year-old sister, Bonnie sitting on the stoop watching me. She had a crayon in her hand and a small pumpkin on her lap.

"I'm gonna' tell on you," she said, drawing on the pumpkin.

"What?" I knocked clumps of dirt off my jeans and pulled twigs out of my hair as I stood up. "What are you going to tell?"

"You're trying to turn into a bat and you know mom won't allow animals in the house."

I hadn't told anyone about my plans to become a bat, so how did she know what I was trying to do? Then it dawned on me—my experiment book.

Last year I'd gotten a chemistry set for Christmas, which was great, except the directions were so hard I couldn't understand how to use it. But at least the set came with a nifty book to record experiments in.

*"You brat!"* I screamed. *"You've been in my stuff!"*

Realizing she'd given herself away, her eyes got big and scared.

"Na, uh." She set the pumpkin down and prepared to run.

"*Fibber!* You read my book!"

"No I didn't…" But she headed for the front door.

"And you *know* what the penalty is for snooping…" I used my meanest voice and came at her with two extended fingers.

"*Mom!*" Bonnie desperately twisted the doorknob. "*Trudy said she's going to pinch me!*"

# 2

Bonnie flung the front door open and ran inside before I could administer her just punishment.

Inside, Mom was busy pinning some kind of fluffy material around my little sister Nellie's waist, and in her rush, Bonnie nearly knocked them both over.

"Watch it, Bonnie!" mom warned. "I almost stuck Nellie with a pin."

"Yeah, *watch it!*" Nellie scolded. "You could have ruined my Halloween costume!"

Nellie's five years old and the baby of the family, so she thinks the world revolves around her.

"Look at me!" she said, shaking her waist like a hula girl. "I'm gonna' be a fairy for Halloween!"

Ignoring her, Bonnie launched into a frantic plea for help. "*Mom*—Trudy said she's going to pinch me!"

"I most certainly did not." I calmly pulled my sweatshirt over my head and hung it on the peg near the front door.

When I act super-calm, it makes me look innocent. "I wasn't being aggressive. I merely told Bonnie that there are consequences for snooping through my stuff."

*"Aggressive"* and *"consequence"* were two new words on my seventh-grade vocabulary list. I was proud of myself for using them both in one sentence. "And besides," I added. "I caught Bonnie drawing on the pumpkins that you got for Jack-O-Lanterns."

Mom ignored both of us and kept on working. Without an audience, Bonnie lost interest in the drama and joined my seven year-old brother Danny in front of the TV.

I snuck up behind her and whispered, *"I'll get you later—snoopy brat!"*

Bonnie pretended like she didn't hear me. But I saw the fear on her face, so I snickered like Snidely Whiplash.


As I watched my mother work on Nellie's Halloween costume it suddenly occurred to me that mom hadn't asked what *I* wanted to be for Halloween.

She'd already put Danny's costume together, which was easy 'cause he was going as a hobo. And Bonnie's costume was an 1800's girl—which was actually my costume from last year's Christmas play. Bonnie, of course, didn't want to wear a hand-me-down, but mom said she'd let Bonnie wear a rhinestone bracelet and necklace with it, and that got her all excited. So now Bonnie is going as an 1800's Jean Harlow.

But this Halloween was special, so I wanted an amazing costume. And with Halloween only two weeks away, mom would need to get started right away.

"How long before you're finished with Nellie's costume?" I asked.

"I'll finish tomorrow." Mom pulled the dress over Nellie's head, careful to avoid sticking her with the straight pins.

"Good, because this year my costume is pretty complex—"

"Oh, Trudy," mom said distractedly. "Don't you think you're a little old to go trick-or-treating?"

Come again?

Was the world just knocked off its axis? Did I just hear her right? I half-expected Rod Serling to say, "And now, you, Trudy McFarlan, have just entered *The Twilight Zone...*"

I swallowed my confusion. "What did you say?"

"I mean, you're in the seventh grade now," mom said, collecting her sewing materials. "Don't you think it's time you stopped dressing up for Halloween?"

I felt like someone had socked me in the gut. I had no breath, I could barely speak. Surely she didn't mean it.

"You're kidding, right?"

"Come on, Trudy, you're not a child anymore and—"

I slammed my hands over my ears and raised my voice. *"Stop saying that! I don't want to hear this—"*

Mom pulled one hand off my ear. "Well, then hear *this*— if you insist on going trick-or-treating like a little kid then you can at least act like a grown-up and make your own costume!"

I was speechless.

I felt like an orphan whose mother had left her in the wilderness to die.

Grow up? Make my own costume?

How on earth do you make a bat costume?

# 3

In my pain and confusion, I marched to my room and slammed the door loudly so everyone would understand that I was in pain and confusion.

This year was not going well.

Not at *all*.

It started out promising when I got permission to spend New Year's Eve at my best friend Paige's house. That night her mom was having a "turning of the decade" party. It was a sophisticated party with champagne and little wieners on toothpicks and other fancy food. Paige and I got to mingle with the guests until 10:00. Then everyone started getting kinda' drunk and her mom made us go to bed. We didn't really go to sleep, just stayed upstairs in Paige's room and watched her Zenith portable TV.

When it was almost midnight we snuck downstairs and swiped some glasses of champagne. Then, at twelve o'clock, we clinked glasses and toasted the New Year—1960—and we drank our wine. It tasted really bad and made me gag. But Paige drank all of hers in one gulp. I think she held her breath when she did it, 'cause she made a really ugly face when she was finished. She wanted me to do the same thing, but it tasted so bad I just couldn't. When she bugged me about it, I said, "Good champagne should be sipped, not gulped." Which was something I'd heard her mother say downstairs.

I pretended to sip my wine but when Paige wasn't looking I dumped the rest of it down the toilet. After a few minutes, Paige got all weird and started saying really stupid stuff, like how she was going to poop on the Zenith portable TV, and other crazy talk. Then suddenly she turned kinda' green and started gagging. I got her to the toilet just in time before she puked up champagne and little wieners.

Then she went to bed and started snoring. I was supposed to sleep next to her, but her puke breath and snoring was so bad I just laid on the floor with a blanket. I got very little sleep that night.

Definitely not the way I wanted to start a new year.

Originally I thought 1960 was going to be a real exciting time—being a new decade and all. I figured it wouldn't be long before we'd all be flying around in spaceships and have two-way wrist radios like Dick Tracy.

But it didn't turn out that way.

Early in the year Paige and I got some disturbing news. We both scored so high on our 5$^{th}$ grade evaluation that we were given a special test to see if we could skip 6$^{th}$ grade and go straight to 7$^{th}$.

Paige liked the idea of skipping a grade. She figured the sooner we got through school the sooner we could open a horse ranch—which is what we planned to do after graduation. And while I liked the idea of spending one less year in the education slammer, I wasn't too thrilled about going to junior high.

For one thing—we'd miss getting to be the school big shots. Six-grade is the highest grade in elementary school, so six graders get to be the bosses of the school and all the younger kids are the peons. We'd been waiting 5 years to become six-graders and if we skipped a grade we wouldn't be Elementary School big shots, we'd be Jr. High peons.

But Paige said it would be okay because we'd be together and we could stick up for each other. Although I begged and pleaded, Paige still refused to fail the test on purpose. And I couldn't very well fail if Paige was going to pass, because then we'd go to different schools and that would be just awful. No matter what else happened, Paige and I had to stick together.

As luck would have it, we both scored really high on the test. We scored with high-school level reading and vocabulary. That's 'cause we both like big words and share new ones with each other all the time and we're both big readers. Our math and science scores were also high enough to skip a grade, so we both jumped from 5th grade and went straight to 7th.

I didn't like leaving my friends at elementary school, but I'd still be in the same class as my buddy Paige.

At least, I thought I would.

But then our evil 5th grade teacher, Mrs. Johnson stuck her big nose in everything and messed that up too.

Mrs. Johnson had a grudge against me for something I did last Christmas. I kinda' showed her up in the Christmas play and, although I made her look like a big comedy star, she still resented my making the audience laugh at her.

To get even with me, Mrs. Johnson recommended that Paige and I be split up and put in separate 7th grade classes.

And that's exactly what happened.

So even though Paige and I were in the same school, we were in different homerooms. And while we both had the same teachers for English and Math, our classes were at different times, so we were never together.

So much for being able to stick up for each other.

No, this year was not going well. And now, with my mother saying stuff about not going trick-or-treating anymore, I was beginning to seriously hate 1960.

# 4

The next day after school I dropped my schoolbooks at home, changed into my grubby jeans and grabbed my rusty little wagon loaded with empty soda pop bottles. Paige and I collect pop bottles and once a week we trade them in for the deposit. For every pop bottle we turn in we get 2¢ and we spend the money on candy.

I'd had a good week collecting bottles. There's a spot at the end of Providence road where all the teenagers hang out and they must have had a big shindig last Saturday 'cause I found a dozen bottles lying in the grass. If Paige also had a good week, we'd be up to our ears in candy.

I rolled the wagon down to Paige's house. Paige's mom doesn't like us to pull a wagon down the street to the store. She says it makes us look like a couple of rag pickers, so we only go on Tuesdays when Mrs. H. is at her bridge club. I was happy to see her car wasn't in the driveway. Mrs. H. doesn't like me very much. She pretends like she does, but she doesn't pretend too hard, so I'm always glad when I don't have to be around her.

Mrs. H. gives Paige everything she wants. That's because Paige is an only child and since Mrs. H.'s husband died when Paige was a little kid, Paige is probably going to stay an only child. So Mrs. H. spoils Paige with everything except candy. Paige's mom says it will rot her teeth and spoil her figure when she gets older, so she withholds sweets. This is part of the reason why Paige comes with me on Tuesday. I think the other reason is because Paige just likes defying her mother.

But it's different with me. My mom and dad can't afford to give me candy-money and they approve of my making my own moola to pay for things mom calls, *nonessentials.*

As I rolled up to Paige's house, she must have seen me coming 'cause she came out of the house. She looked at the wagon and made a strange face. "I see you found a bunch of bottles."

"Sure did!"

"I don't have any. My mom's on a diet so she's not drinking any Coke."

"That's okay, I've got 12, so that's 24¢, enough for a Zero bar, a Hershey's bar and two Pixie Stiks. We can split the candy bars in half, and it'll be like we've two each."

"That'll work."

We started walking down the street and the wagon was clinking like one of those little glass wind chimes they sell at the dime store. As far as I'm concerned, there's no prettier sound on earth than a wagon full of pop bottles. But Paige kept glancing at the wagon like it was annoying her.

My mom calls me and Paige *frick and frack* because we look so different. I've got brown hair, brown eyes and I'm an average size girl while Paige has light blonde hair, blue eyes and she's smaller.

Paige's size is what my mom calls d*elicate,* although Paige is anything but. I once saw her grab a boy six inches taller than her and slam him into a telephone pole. Then she threatened to bash his face in if he didn't stop calling her *bubble bean.* That was last year when her mom gave her a Tony perm and her hair was all curly. The boy knew she was serious about the face-bashing so he shut up real fast.

I glanced over at Paige and noticed that her perm had almost grown out. Good thing, too. She really did look like a bubble bean.

"Guess what, Trudy?"

"What?"

"This will be the last time we return pop bottles for money."

"You're kidding, right?"

"Serious as a preacher's corpse."

"How come?"

"Starting next week my mom's giving me 75¢ a week for allowance."

"Whoa! How did you get her to do that?"

"It was her idea. She said since I'm in Jr. High now, I'm going to need spending money for stuff like fingernail polish and lace handkerchiefs—"

*"What!"*

Paige and I made a pact last year to never be girly-girls. Since there are no girl astronauts, forest rangers, or other cool jobs like that, we figured if we never gave in to being girly-girls we would be able to do the same stuff as boys.

"I'm not going to spend my allowance on stuff like that—I just let my mom think I would."

*"Whew!* For a minute I thought you'd become a turncoat."

"Yeah…well," Paige kind of hesitated and it made me wonder what she was thinking. "Anyway, now we don't have to collect pop bottles anymore. We can spend my allowance on candy."

The truth was, I *liked* collecting pop bottles. It was like treasure hunting. "Thanks for the offer, but I don't want to sponge off you."

"Then why don't you ask your parents for an allowance?"

"I did." I shuffled my feet, kicking some dried leaves off the road. "I asked my dad for an allowance once, but he said every time I sit down to dinner I'm eating my allowance."

"Oh."

We walked along in silence, and I was about to tell Paige that I didn't want to stop collecting pop bottles, when suddenly her face split into a big grin.

"But here's the *really* good news! You know that Halloween party you and I have always dreamed of having?"

Paige and I have talked about having a Halloween party ever since we were in the second grade. Every year we'd go to the store and choose the decorations, then plan the games, the music and even the food. And while other girls planned their perfect wedding, Paige and I planned the perfect Halloween party.

But it was just a fantasy. We never got to have the party of our dreams.

"Are you saying what I think you're saying?"

"That's right! This year mom is going to let us have a Halloween party!"

"No lie?"

"No lie—which means we can have a party on Saturday, October 29th, then go trick or treating on Monday—so it'll be like having *two* Halloweens!"

19

"That's fantastic!"

"And it gets even better—mom's going to buy all the refreshments, but she's giving me a budget of $8 to spend on decorations!"

"That's too cool! We finally get to buy all the stuff we've been drooling over!"

"I know, *right?* We can go to McCory's next week and get some black cats, skeletons arms and legs that move, wax lips and plastic witches—"

"And orange and black crepe-paper!" There's something about crepe-paper streamers that's so darn festive. I think it's an absolute *must* for any party. "Oh! And lets not forget the most important thing—bats."

"Bats?"

"Sure! We've got to get a bunch of those rubber bats that you hang from the ceiling to make it look like they're flying around the room." I hadn't told Paige I was going to be a bat for Halloween, so it would be a big surprise when I showed up in a bat costume and had those rubber bats flying all around me like my evil henchmen.

"Yeah, bats would be cool." Paige didn't sound too excited about bats, although it was an absolute *must.*

"So, how many people can we invite?"

"Mom said not to invite more than fourteen. We're having the party in our basement and the rec-room won't hold too many kids, what with all the refreshments and party stuff an' all."

"Well, that's plenty of kids!" I thought of all the friends we left behind in Elementary school. It would be great to get them all together again. It would be like Paige and I were still in 5$^{th}$ grade. "We can invite all our friends from last year and—"

"Actually...I planned on inviting mostly kids from Junior High." Paige dropped her eyes and kicked some gravel off the road.

"Okay...but not *all*—I mean, you're going to invite Nancy and Doris Simms, Arlene Rueter, Mark Clark and—"

"Um...maybe." She started fidgeting with the hem of her shirt. "You see, one of the girl's in my class is putting together a list of all the kids we need to invite—"

*"Need* to invite?"

"Yeah, well...she's helping me stay out of *The Cootie Catchers.*"

"The what?"

*"The Cootie Catchers*—it's what the really unpopular kids are called. You know—the dregs, the grody kids, the

ones with the *Kick Me* signs on their backs. The ones that dress kind of dorky..."

I knew exactly who she was talking about.

We all sat at the same lunch table every day.

Some of the kids who sat at the table dressed nice, but they were awkward, so they got the *Kick Me!* signs taped to their backs. Then there were the kids like me who didn't own expensive clothes like cashmere sweaters, or tartan skirts with the big gold safety pin on the side. And we didn't wear the newest shoes like penny loafers or saddle shoes.

Kids who dress dorky? Well, that would certainly be me. Most of my clothes were cranked out of my mother's sewing machine. Mom wasn't the best seamstress, so some of my blouses had crooked collars and the patterns on my dresses rarely lined up. The elastic in most of my knee-high socks was stretched out, so my socks were usually down around my ankles. And it didn't matter how scruffy my shoes were, as long as there was leather between my foot and the ground, I didn't get new ones.

I knew I wasn't the best-dressed kid in the school.

I just didn't know I was called a *Cootie Catcher.*

# 5

I dropped the handle on my wagon, put my hand on my hip and faced Paige.

"Are you talking about *me?*"

"What? *Of course not!*" Paige's eyes got real big so I knew she was telling the truth. "I'm talking about, you know...someone like Miriam Langston."

Miriam Langston lives in our neighborhood. She's two years older than us, but she was kept back a grade so she started 7<sup>th</sup> grade the same time Paige and I did.

Miriam is the neighborhood tormentor. She's big and pushy and one time she even sat on me and made me eat dirt.

"Yeah, what about her?"

"Well, you know how tough she's always been?"

"Yeah..."

"Well, she's in my homeroom and she's at the bottom of the barrel. The other kids make fun of her and even do stuff like push her in the boy's lavatory."

"Really?"

"I know, *right?* Remember in 6<sup>th</sup> grade how she used to walk around the hallways like she owned the school? Well, now she just kind of *skulks* through the hallways. She has almost *no* friends."

Miriam rides our school bus, and it suddenly occurred to me that she was always sitting by herself. I guess Paige was right. Junior high had reduced the mighty Miriam to a schoolyard wuss.

"So…here's the thing…I have to do stuff to fit in with everyone else because I don't want to end up with *Kick Me!* signs on my back. You understand, right?"

Paige never worried about stuff like that before. I mean, we might not have been the most popular kids in elementary school, but then we never tried to be either. We were just regular kids. And it seemed kind of weird that now she had to worry about fitting in.

"Anyway, Cassandra is one of the cool kids and she said that since I'm clever and dress really nice an' all, I have a good chance of getting into *The Big Eight.*

"The big eight?"

"Yeah, that's the eight most popular kids in the 7th grade. Cassandra said if you get into The Big Eight in 7th grade it'll carry you all the way through Junior High and you'll never get picked on."

Now this was really weird. Paige and I went to the same Jr. High, and we were in the same grade, but I never even heard of *Cootie Catchers* or *The Big Eight.*

"So, how does Cassandra know all this?"

"Her older sister was one of The Big Eight before she went to High School." Paige lifted her face and it looked like she had a stomachache. "The main thing is—I don't want to become one of the Cootie Catchers. They get treated really mean, and since I'm a year younger than everyone else in my class, all the kids started calling me braniac, shrimp, peanut, and other stuff, and it would be real easy for me to become one of the cooties. But then Cassandra started helping me and I began to get accepted."

"But, Paige…we've been planning this Halloween party since we were little kids. Now you're going to let someone else do the inviting? This was supposed to be *our* party."

"Don't worry, it'll still be *our* party. We'll just have some new kids there, that's all."

We walked along in silence as I digested this information.

*Digest information* is a term my English teacher, Mr. Harmon, uses when we're supposed to think about something new.

But this information was giving me indigestion.

# 6

Paige allowing Cassandra to invite a bunch of new kids to the party had me kind of rattled. I mean, I knew there were different groups of kids in Jr. High; some rich, some poor, some popular, some not—but I didn't know we were given names like *Cootie Catchers, Cool Kids*, or *The Big Eight*.

I thought about all the kids I hung out with in school and it occurred to me that we just kind of gravitated toward each other. We didn't sit together at lunch because we had signs on our foreheads that said what group we were in, we just hung out because we were friendly, or had stuff to talk about. I hated the idea of having to stop and think what group a kid was in before I sat next to them. From the sound of things, I didn't think I'd fit in with the kids Paige was inviting. Especially since I didn't dress like them.

But then…we'd all be in costumes, so who would know? I mean, who was going to know that I was one of the kids who wore dorky clothes to school?

I thought about how cool my bat costume was going to be. I hadn't told Paige about it because I wanted the costume to be a big surprise. I imagined myself showing up at her party as a giant bat with bloody fangs and terrifying all those kids from her class. Who knows, they might even cry and wet their pants. Then no one would ever bother Paige at school because they'd all be afraid of her vampire bat friend. And Paige wouldn't need Cassandra anymore.

That would be so cool.

Okay, maybe it was a little farfetched, but the idea still had merit.

So, I made up mind.

I would make the best bat costume the world had ever seen. It would be so cool and so scary that those Jr. High kids would never call anyone a Cootie Catcher, stick notes on kid's backs, or shove anyone in the boy's lavatory again, because if they did, they'd incur the wrath of *the bat*. And because it was a costume party, they'd never know who the bat was in real life.

And that's what made it so scary—the bat could be *anyone.*

And it might actually work because that's the magic of Halloween—unlimited potential.

Halloween has no restrictions, no rules, no obstacles to being whatever you want to be. A skinny kid can be fat, a wimpy kid can be Superman, a city kid can be a cowboy—no limits, just pure potential.

But did a super cool bat costume have the potential to change the Jr. High caste system?

Maybe not, but sometimes I do things I know are impossible and I do them anyway because there's always the teeniest, tiniest chance that they might be possible. And if a girl doesn't try, she'll never find out for sure.

And this was one of those times.

# 7

**Gilbert Chemistry Set Experiment Book**

**Date:** *Friday, October 21, 1960*

**Experiment Objective:** *Make super cool bat costume.*

### Steps:

**1.** *Gathering stuff together for bat body; black tights for legs. The tights are mine from last year, so they're a little small and the crotch sags, but that's okay because a bat's body is kinda' baggy anyway.*

**2.** *Will use my sweatshirt with the hood as the bat's upper body. My sweatshirt is red, so I have to dye it black. I know mom has some black dye around here somewhere.*

**3.** *Found it! A half bottle of Ritz's fabric dye was stored under the kitchen sink. I took it and hid it in my bedroom.*

**4.** *Found my old mittens from last winter. Will use them as ears. They're red, so they must also be dyed black. The directions on the dye don't look too hard, but I'll have to wait until mom is out of the house or she'll stop me. She goes food shopping next week. I'll do it then.*

**Result:** *Got body together, now must find super cool batwings.*

I searched around the house for something to use as batwings, but there was nothing. Our house is decorated in Early American junk, so there's plenty of revolutionary soldiers, stars & stripes, and green plaid, but nothing bat worthy.

Luckily, tomorrow is trash day and since people put their trash out the night before, I figured I'd ride my bike around and look for something with batwing potential.

Mom forbids me to dig through other people's trash, but this is an emergency. And besides, what mom doesn't know won't hurt her.

Grabbing my bike, I walked it up the driveway to begin searching for those perfect batwings.

At the top of the hill is my dad's business. He owns a service station where he fixes people's cars and sells gas. He runs the business pretty much by himself, but my grandpa helps out by pumping gas and running to Joppa Auto for parts.

When I got to the top of the hill, I saw my Aunt Katie's car at the gas pump and grandpa preparing to fill her tank. I love pumping gas, and since it was still pretty early for scouting trash, I put my bike down and ran over.

"Hey, Aunt Katie—can I put the gas in your car?"

My Aunt Katie is my only adult friend. Her husband died when I was just a baby so Aunt Katie lives alone. The neighbors think she's a little crazy but she's not really. It's just that Aunt Katie doesn't tolerate fools and she's not afraid to tell people so. And because of that, people think she's a little touched. But when I grow up I want to be just like my Aunt Katie—a widow who doesn't take crap off nobody.

"Sure Trudy, you can put gas in my car."

"I don't think she can, Kate." Grandpa glanced nervously at the garage.

"Of course she can! Any darn fool can pump gas."

"I know she *can*, but…"

Grandpa was worried about my dad because dad thinks girls shouldn't do gas station stuff. If dad caught me pumping gas, he'd yell at me *and* grandpa. And Grandpa hates for people to yell at him.

"Well…I guess it's okay. Her dad's in the pit."

The pit is a square hole in the garage floor with stairs that go to the bottom. Dad parks a car on top of the pit when he has to work under the car. I used to scare my sister Nellie by telling her a monster lived in the pit. But when mom heard me she made me tell Nellie the truth.

"Okay, Trudy," Grandpa handed me the nozzle. "But don't spill any. If you go home smelling like gas, you're dad will really jack me up."

I grabbed the gas nozzle and waited while grandpa cranked the dollar numbers back to zero. Then I put the nozzle in the car and began pumping. I like the smell of gas and watching the wavy fumes come out of the tank, so I was really enjoying myself, when suddenly a bear growled. *"Great googamooga! What's going on out here?"*

Grandpa and I both jumped. And grandpa quickly grabbed the nozzle from my hand.

*"Trudy!* How many times have do I have to tell you to stay away from that gas pump?"

My dad was standing at the garage door. He started marching toward us until he remembered the cigarette in his mouth and he stopped.

"Oh, Dale," Aunt Katie yelled back. "She's just helping—"

"I don't want to hear that! And *Pop,"* he pointed at grandpa with his cigarette. "You know I don't want kids near those pumps!"

I figured I better high-tail it out of there before dad told me to go home and help my mom clean. Which is what he always does when he catches me doing something he doesn't like.

*"Sorry, dad!"* I yelled and made a dash for my bike.

"Trudy—" he started to say something but I didn't stop, just yelled over my shoulder, *"Bye Aunt Katie!"*

"—girls don't pump gas! *You got that?"*

I pretended like I didn't hear as I sped down the road on my bike. It really bugs me that my dad always says girls can't do stuff.

I bet he wouldn't talk like that to a big scary bat with bloody fangs.

## 8

I rode up and down Providence Road passing houses decorated for Halloween. The Hutchinson's had a cardboard skeleton on their door and their neighbor had cardboard witches and cats in the windows. The Jacobs family had a bunch of white handkerchiefs with black eyes drawn on them to look like ghosts dangling from the tree limbs. People with no imagination just put dried corn on their door, but it was still cool to see everyone gearing up for Halloween.

Seeing all the decorations reminded me I only had a week to get my costume together. Feeling the pressure, I pumped the pedals of my bike with new determination, speeding down the road and carefully checking every open trashcan. But there was nothing bat-worthy on Providence Road.

Expanding my search, I turned into the Pineleigh housing development. And as I was riding up Roxleigh Road, I spotted something at the top of the hill that made my heart flutter. A large black umbrella was turned inside out and sticking out the top of a trashcan.

*Batwings!*

The umbrella was perfect! It had everything I needed. It had flexible material that was kind of leathery looking and it had umbrella spokes that looked like batwing bones. It was like the Halloween spirits had led me to that very trashcan!

I began pedaling faster up the hill, but before I could get to the trashcan, the door to the house next door opened and Justin Palladino walked out.

Justin is a new kid in the neighborhood. He's fourteen years old, has sandy brown hair, buckteeth and wears glasses. He looks a little like Arnold Stang who's the guy that does the Nestle Chunky Chocolate commercials and says, *"What a chunk of chocolate!"* But Justin is taller and cuter.

Now here's the thing, I secretly like three guys. My first true love is Sherlock Holmes, but since he's not a real person, he just stays in my imagination. The other person is Arnold Stang. I like his glasses 'cause they make him look smart and I like smart guys. I also like that Arnold Stang is a little guy, but fearless. He never backs down from anyone. And, unlike Sherlock Holmes,

Arnold Stang is a real person. However, he's someone I'll probably never meet, so he stays in my imagination too.

But then there's Justin Palladino.

You'd think that someone with buckteeth and glasses would be kind of nerdy and awkward, but he's not. He's a very confident guy. Not only that, for a fourteen year-old, he's nice to everyone—which most teenagers aren't. He's also very smart and goes to Loyola, which is a private school for smart kids and very expensive. Justin is so smart that he's already in high school.

Justin moved to Pineleigh last year and was immediately accepted by all the neighborhood kids. Justin joined our baseball games and sat around afterward when it got dark and looked at the stars with the rest of us. It didn't seem to bother him that he was a high school teenager while the rest of us were either in elementary or Jr. High. He's very confident that way.

One time I knew he was going to be at a neighborhood ballgame, so put on mom's cologne called *Wild Summer!* But when I got to the game, two boys started making fun of me.

There are two guys in the neighborhood who are just plain rotten. Melvin, who's in the 5$^{th}$ grade and his brother Jacob who's in the 4$^{th}$ grade. We call them the Smelly brothers. Their real name is spelled *Smellie* and they say it's supposed to be pronounced Smeel-lee, but everyone just calls them the Smellys—Melvin and Jacob Smelly.

I was embarrassed because they were making fun of me. I didn't want anyone to know I wore the cologne so Justin would notice me, and I was afraid the Smellys would guess and start saying something juvenile like, *Trudy and Justin sitting in tree, K-I-S-S-I-N-G...*

But Justin shut them up by saying, "She's a girl. She's *supposed* to smell better than us stinky boys."

"Yeah, but who wears perfume to play baseball?" Melvin wouldn't let it go. He was still trying to embarrass me.

But Justin just looked at him and said, "Well, maybe if you wore aftershave to the ballgame you'd be able to hit the ball as good as she does."

Everyone thought that was pretty clever and started laughing. Then Justin turned his back to everyone and winked at me.

It was the first time anyone had ever defended me.

And it made my legs feel like they were made of Jell-O.

So, when Justin Palladino walked out the front door and stood between me and my batwings, I couldn't...I mean, I just *couldn't* let him see me digging in a trashcan!

# 9

I figured I would ride my bike around until Justin went back in the house, then I'd get the umbrella out of the trash.

I watched Justin walk to his front yard and pick a newspaper up off the lawn. As he straightened up he saw me and yelled, "Hey, Trudy!" And he waved the paper to get my attention.

"Hey, Justin!" I slowed down and stopped in front of his house.

Justin walked over to my bike and smiled at me.

I get kind of flustered around Justin so I said the first thing I could think of. "Getting your daily dose of news, I see." As soon as I said it I realized how stupid it sounded.

But Justin just smiled and said, "Oh, you know...current events homework. Have to get some information on the Kennedy/Nixon debate that's going to be televised tomorrow night. Do you have a favorite in this election?

Out of the corner of my eye I noticed the Smelly brothers walking down the street and that kind of distracted me.

"Uh...favorite?" I was leaning toward Kennedy, but I wanted to hear what Justin had to say first. "I'm...uh... waiting until the last debate before I make up my mind."

"Smart." He nodded with approval. "My mom said she's going to vote for Kennedy just because he's so handsome. I don't think that's a good reason to vote for anyone. I think character is more important than looks..."

I was upset to see the Smellys spot the umbrella and run toward it, pushing each other out of the way as they went.

"...but that being said, I think Kennedy has a lot of character," Justin continued. "Nixon, however, has a lot of experience. This is going to be a tough election."

"My mom also thinks Kennedy is handsome," I said absentmindedly, praying the Smellys wouldn't grab my umbrella. "But I don't know what she sees in him. I guess when you compare him to Nixon or Eisenhower he's handsome, so maybe for a *politician* he's cute, but he'd never get his own TV show or anything..."

Glancing up the street I saw Melvin Smelly grab the umbrella and start jabbing his brother with it. I sent a silent message to Smelly Mellie, *drop the umbrella, drop the umbrella...*

Following my gaze, Justin watched the Smellys battling over the broken umbrella. "Those boys," he chuckled. "Can you imagine? Playing with an old piece of junk like that!"

"Kids!" I tried to sound like an adult. "What imaginations!" But I was heartbroken that they had my batwings.

We both watched as Jacob and Melvin ran down the street with the umbrella. Before they got out of sight, Jacob took it away from his brother and smacked him on the head with it. Watching them fight over that umbrella I knew there was no way I would ever get it away from them.

"Speaking of playing," Justin said, bringing me back. "I don't think this nice weather's going to last much longer, so I'm getting everyone together for one last ballgame on Sunday. Are you in?"

"Of course."

"Good," he said, walking back to his house. "I'll see you then!" When he got to the entrance, he smiled at me before closing the door.

One last ballgame?

Those words settled on me and I suddenly realized it would probably be the last time I'd get to spend time with Justin until spring. Once winter set in there would be no excuse to get together except for the occasional snowball battle or to go sledding—and even then, there was no guarantee that Justin would be there. By spring he'd be fifteen and he might even be too old to play ball with the neighborhood kids anymore.

A strange kind of pain suddenly wrapped itself around my heart.

And I desperately wished summer would never end.

# 10

**Gilbert Chemistry Set Experiment Book**

**Date:** *Saturday, October 22, 1960*

**Experiment Objective:** *Can't find anything to make my costume with so I'll have to buy something. Must get some money!*

### Steps:

**1.** *I went through all the old, rusted-out cars that dad uses for parts at the service station. I slid my hand deep into each seat. I came out with 69¢.*

**2.** *I did the same thing at our house with the sofa and chair. Mom saw me doing it and said, "Don't bother. How do you think I paid the milkman?" Since mom had already drained the sofa, I gave up.*

**3.** *I swept Grandma's porch and raked the leaves in her yard. It was hard work, so I figured she'd give me at least 75¢, but she only gave me 10¢. Grandma thinks that's big moola. When I made a face she told me a long, windy story about when she was a kid and a dime being enough to buy a Rolls Royce or something stupid like that. I really didn't listen.*

**Result:** *Have got 79¢ to buy material for costume. Also learned not to do hard work for old people.*

Paige's mom is taking us to McCrory's today to buy fabric for Paige's costume. We're also going to buy decorations for the Halloween party. But while we're in the fabric department, I'll see if I have enough money for batwing material.

I waited at my dad's service station for Paige's mom to pick me up. His service station has a big paved entrance that leads from the road to the gas pumps. Since it was Saturday there are loads of cars going to Loch Raven to see the leaves turn color. Those leaf-watchers are so busy looking at the treetops it's not safe to stand anywhere near the road, so I waited near the pumps.

Paige's mom was early, so I was glad I was there waiting. If Paige would've had to go find me, Mrs. H. would have been hopping mad. The only time Mrs. H. likes me is when she's drinking sparkling burgundy. But since it wasn't even lunchtime, I didn't think that would be the case.

I opened the back door of Mrs. H.'s Lincoln Continental and was shocked to find an unfamiliar girl in the back seat. It took me a second, but I finally realized who it was. *"Paige?* Is that you?"

"Yep!" she said, grinning from ear to ear. "Don't you just *love* it?"

Paige's hair was cut really, really, *really* short and it made her look like a different person. With all the blond hair cut away from her face, her eyes looked super big and blue. It also made her lips look bigger and her face kind of delicate.

This was not the Paige I knew.

"It's called a *pixie cut,*" Mrs. H. said from the front seat. "My hairdresser said it's the latest thing, and Paige said no one in junior high is wearing this style yet, so Paige will be a *trendsetter!*"

"What do you think, Trudy?" Paige looked kind of worried when she asked. I didn't want to make her feel bad, because, unless there was a formula to grow hair super fast, she couldn't change back to the old Paige.

"It's...neat." I forced a smile. "I mean, it takes a minute to get used to, but it kind of makes you look like...oh, I don't know..."

*"Tinker Bell!"* she said, running her fingers through what was left of her hair. "And that's who I'm going to be for Halloween! Mom's even going to have the Chinese woman who does her sewing make me some fairy wings and a costume like Tinker Bell's. Cool, huh?"

"Boy, howdy..." I pretended to be enthusiastic.

The new haircut made Paige look pretty and cool and everything, so I should have been happy for her. But there was something about this change that I just didn't like.

I mean...why would Paige want to be Tinker Bell for Halloween when she could just as easily be Peter Pan?

# 11

When we got to McCroy's Mrs. H. gave Paige a ten dollar bill and said, "Don't forget, I get two dollars in change."

"But mom," Paige stuck the bill in her pocket. "You forgot that I have to buy invitations for the party. That isn't part of my decorations budget. I'm going to need that extra two dollars."

"You're not fooling me, Paige Marie Haussman, invitations only cost 29¢. Just make sure you bring me change." Mrs. H. sounded annoyed. "And don't get any of those invitations with monsters on them. Make sure you get tasteful ones—after all, you're in junior high now."

"It's *Halloween,* mom!" Paige imitated her mother's annoyance. "Not one of your fancy dinner parties!"

"Just get your things and meet me at the cash register." Before she walked away, Mrs. H. looked at me and scowled like it was my fault Paige back-talks her.

"Grab one of those hand baskets, Trudy." Paige pointed to the basket rack. "No, make it two. We're going to get a lot of stuff, now that we've got ten dollars to spend."

"But, your mom said—"

"When we're done I'll hand her some coins. She won't count then, so she'll never know."

Things are sure different at Paige's house. My mom knows every penny she's supposed to get back in change.

"Okay..." Paige pulled a piece of paper out of her pocket. "I made a list. First, let's start with a paper table cloth..."

It was like a dream come true! All the years Paige and I planned our party, what we would buy and how we would decorate, and now we were actually doing it! This would be a Halloween I'd never forget!

Paige and I went down the bins of Halloween stuff and filled our baskets with paper plates decorated with black cats, orange napkins and we even got a Beistal centerpiece—a flat paper moon and witch that folded out into a tissue paper honeycomb.

Next, we started gathering wall decorations—skeletons, cats, witches and ghosts, and—of course—

orange and black crepe paper streamers—a must for *any* party.

As we walked along perusing the decorations, I glanced up and saw the most important decoration of all—rubber bats!

"Paige—I found them! How many do you think we should get?"

"Um…I don't know if we have enough money for that," she said, looking through the baskets we held.

"I've been keeping count—we've only spent $3.80—we've got lots of money left!"

"Yeah…but I still have to get the contest prizes and some 45 records and…"

"Records? You mean like spooky Halloween sounds?"

"No, I mean like Chubby Checker's new record."

"But… he's not scary."

"It's for the dance contest. We're all going to do that new dance *the Twist*, and whoever does it best wins a prize."

Dance contest? In all our years of planning, Paige and I had never talked about having a dance contest. "You mean whoever twists in the most grotesque way will win a prize?"

"No, I mean regular dancing." She walked away from the hanging bats without even giving them a second look. "That's what we do at Jr. High parties, Trudy—we dance."

Paige said it in such a snobby way it made me wonder if that new hairdo hadn't done something to her brain.

"Okay...but we're still going to do the other stuff, like bobbing for apples and telling ghost stories, and—"

"Well,...maybe. I have to check with Cassandra first."

*"Cassandra?"* I felt like the top of my head was going to blow off. "Since when is this *Cassandra's* party?"

"It's not like it's *her* party..." Paige dropped her chin and looked at the floor. "It's just that she wrote out the guest list and she knows whether or not the kids would like our games or not, and..."

"Gee, I'm surprised that Cassandra allowed you to come to your own party." I said it in a real snotty way so Paige would get the point. "I mean, did Cassandra let you invite *anyone* to your own party?"

"She let me invite you," Paige said quietly.

"She *let* you?"

I was flabbergasted.

The very idea of a Halloween party without me was unthinkable! This was our dream—Paige and mine—not *Cassandra's!* And Paige was acting like I was that dorky kid your mom forces you to invite to your birthday party.

It was just too much!

I was on the verge of giving Miss Paige Marie Haussman a piece of my mind, when she took my arm and said, "And…and you get to invite someone too! And it can be anyone you like…"

I could tell this was a peace offering but I was so mad I didn't care. And I was just about to tell Paige what she could do with her invitation, when an idea suddenly hit me so hard it felt like a lightening bolt went through my brain.

I could invite anyone I wanted.

Even Justin Palladino.

# 12

I was quiet as we walked through the store to meet up with Paige's mother. I kept thinking about inviting Justin to the Halloween party.

It was an exciting idea.

For one thing, I'd get to see him at a party instead of just at the ball field. It would be more like we were *friends*. And mom always said that when someone invites you to something you had an obligation to return their invitation. If I invited Justin to this party, he would have to invite me to something, too. For sure.

But what would he invite me to?

I tried to imagine what went on in Justin's life. A church thing maybe?

I was pretty sure he was Catholic. He had a dirt smudge on his forehead last March, and he said it was 'cause of Ash Wednesday. I'm pretty sure only Catholics rub dirt on their faces before Easter.

So, what kind of socials does the Catholic Church have?

They eat fish on Friday—so, maybe a fish fry? Would Justin invite me to something like that?

I hope not. I hate fish.

Maybe something at his school? A football game? A basketball game? And maybe, just maybe…a dance. Would he even be allowed to bring an eleven year-old to a dance? But then, he didn't have to tell anyone how old I was. And I could wear my hair in upsweep to look older—it's long enough now. Mom let me grow my hair out because I'm old enough to take care of it myself and she doesn't have to comb out the tangles anymore. My hair is now down to my shoulders—long enough for an upsweep hairdo.

I mean, I wouldn't do it to be girly or anything. I would just wear my hair like that as a kind of *disguise.* And Justin would know I was in disguise and it would be our private joke. Maybe we'd even tell people I was related to Annette Funicello, or something.

Yeah, it could work.

I was suddenly glad that we had to learn how to dance in physical education class. I wasn't good at it, but at least I knew how to do the cha cha, the foxtrot and the Madison. I made a mental note to start watching the Buddy Deane show after school so I could learn all the new teenage dances. If I was going to go to his school as Annette Funicello's relative, everyone would expect me to dance.

The thought of dancing brought me back to the Halloween party. Now that Justin would be invited to the party, I would probably dance with him. The very idea of dancing with Justin was kind of scary. But kind of not.

However...would I be able to do the Twist in a bat costume?

I didn't want to give up the bat costume, but maybe I needed to change it a little. I was now glad I didn't get that umbrella for the bat wings. The umbrella spokes would have been too stiff for me to do the Twist, and I needed something that could bend.

The idea of my bat costume began to change in my mind. I saw my fingernails painted red—not to be girly or anything—but red is a good color for bat fingernails. Maybe even some red lipstick. I'd never seen a bat up close but it seemed to me they had red mouths. And I was pretty sure they had long eyelashes—so maybe I'd used mom's eyelash curler.

But instead of leathery wings, I was now starting to see the wings made out of something softer.

Black lace?

*Heck no!* For one thing mom would never let me out of the house in anything made of black lace! I suddenly thought of the naughty calendar dad keeps in his service station and the girl in the black lace nightgown, and I felt my face turn red.

Definitely not black lace. But what about chiffon?

As though reading my mind, Paige suddenly said, "*Chiffon!* Oh mom, I love it!"

We got to the front of the store at the same time Mrs. H finished paying for the material.

"We'll make your fairy wings out of the chiffon," she said leading us to the parking lot. "And we'll sew sequins on the body of the costume, and…"

As we got to the car, it suddenly occurred to me that I'd been so busy thinking about inviting Justin to the party that I'd completely forgotten to get material for my own costume.

And the rubber bats.

I'd forgotten them too.

# 13

I spent an hour practicing my cursive writing before I wrote on Justin's invitation. I wanted to write it in ink, but mom's fountain pen was dry and we didn't have any ink cartridges so I had to use a pencil—which was only one step above a crayon, but it would have to do.

After I had it written, I combed my hair, put on a pair of jeans with no holes, and splashed on some of mom's *My Sin* cologne. Then I got on my bike and headed to Justin's house.

I thought about giving him the invitation at the ball game, but I was afraid the Smellys would see me do it and say something to embarrass me. Plus I was also afraid if I thought about it overnight I would chicken out and not give Justin the invitation at all.

All the way to his house I worried about what he would say when he read it. Would he smile and say he'd *love* to come? Or would he laugh at me and say, *No way!* My stomach got all knotted up just thinking about it.

As my bike got closer to his house, I became more and more convinced that he wouldn't come to the party. I mean, after all, he's a high school boy. True, he got bumped up a few grades, but still, high school boys aren't like everyone else—they're more untouchable. If I gave him the invitation he would probably just laugh at me, or pat me on the head like dog and say, "Oh, that's cute, little girl—*but I don't think so!*"

By the time I got to Justin's street I was so scared just thinking about knocking on his door that I almost turned back. And even when I saw Justin in the driveway washing a car, I was still too scared to give him the invitation.

Because I knew he wouldn't want to come.

And I knew he would make fun of me for inviting him. I just *knew it.*

But then…sometimes I do things I know are impossible but I do them anyway because there's always the teeniest, tiniest chance that they might be possible. And if a girl doesn't try, she'll never find out for sure.

I rode my bike to Justin's driveway and when he saw me he waved a soapy sponge and said, "Hey, Trudy!"

"Hey Justin!" I wasn't sure what else to say so I said, "I see you're washing a car." Then I felt super stupid for saying such a dumb thing, because it was obvious he wasn't playing tiddlywinks.

But Justin didn't act like I'd said something stupid. He just smiled and said, "Yeah...my dad pays me to wash his car."

"No kidding? That's a good way to earn money." I thought about all the cars at my dad's service station and realized I'd been sitting on a goldmine my whole life and never knew it.

"Yeah...my dad likes me to earn my own money." Justin said.

"Yeah...my parents are like that too."

We both got kind of quiet and I wasn't sure what else to say, so I got on my bike and said, "Well, I'll let you get back to work."

Justin smiled and waved his sponge as I rode down the driveway. But before I hit the street, it dawned on me that I hadn't given him the invitation. I turned around super fast, and I nearly fell off my bike. Luckily I got my foot down just in time, so instead of looking clumsy, it looked like I'd done it on purpose.

"Cool move," Justin said. "How'd you learn that?"

"Oh, you know...practice," I lied. Then I reached into my sweatshirt pocket, pulled out the invitation. "Here," I said, handing it to him. "I almost forgot to give you this."

His hands were wet so he took it by the corner. "What is it?"

"An invitation to a Halloween party."

"You having a party?"

"Well, me and my friend Paige. We're having it at her house 'cause she's got a finished basement."

He dried his hands on his pants, opened the invitation and read. He took so long reading that I got kind of scared. "It's not a little kid party or anything," I said quickly. "I mean, it's going to be all older kids, so I thought you might want to come."

Justin looked up from the invitation. "I don't have my glasses on, so I can't tell what it says. Is this going to be a costume party?"

"Yeah...but you don't *have* to wear a costume."

"Are you going to wear a costume?"

"Sure...I mean, it's Halloween."

"Yeah, right. So, what're you going to be?"

"Oh, I don't know..." I felt kind of shy telling him. "I was thinking maybe I'd be something like...oh, maybe something like…I don't know, maybe… *a bat."* I said that last part kind of quiet.

"A cat?"

"No…a bat."

"I don't think I've ever seen a bat costume before."

"I'm sure there will be plenty of cats at the party." I was making up stuff as I went along. "So I thought I'd do something different—you know, so I won't look like everyone else."

"Yeah…I get that."

Neither one of us said anything for a long time and it was starting to get really uncomfortable. I figured he didn't want to come and was just trying to think of a good excuse. To fill in the quiet, I picked my bike up off the lawn and dusted off the seat even though there was nothing on it.

"I don't know if I have a costume or not," Justin said. "I mean, I haven't dressed up for Halloween in a long time…"

I got on my bike and put my foot on the pedal, ready to speed away as soon as he turned down the invitation.

"…but I guess I can come up with something," he said. "Sounds like fun. I'll be there."

I was grinning so hard I must have looked like a clown, so I forced the smile off my face and said, "Yeah…fun."

"Yeah…fun." He picked up his sponge and went back to the car.

I began pedaling down the driveway, when Justin yelled out, "Hey, Trudy—maybe I'll come as Dracula!"

And I felt that stupid smile spread all over my face again.

# 14

I didn't get much sleep that night. I kept thinking about Paige's party and how important it was for my costume to be both cool *and* scary.

It had to be scary so Paige would understand that she didn't need help from dumb girls like Cassandra. She wouldn't need Cassandra anymore because my costume would be so scary that the kids at Paige's party would have no choice but to respect anyone who was friends with the fearsome bat. And not only was it important for Paige, but for every dorky kid who went to Towsontown Jr. High. If I could instill the right amount of fear, there would be no more calling kids *Cootie Catchers,* no more *Kick Me!* signs, no more shoving innocent hall-walkers into lavatories. Okay, maybe it was a lot to expect from a bat costume, but it was the only idea I had.

And of course, my costume had to be cool.

Now that I was going to the party with Justin—him dressed as Dracula and me as the world's most feared bat—

we would fill the room with our coolness so we had to be both feared and *envied.*

The stakes had been raised.

It was now deadly important for me to come up with a spectacular costume.

Sequins on the wings? Would that be cool or scary?

That is, if I had wings.

The Halloween party was less than a week away, so I had to come up with a costume really fast.

But how?


I woke up Sunday morning to the sound of rain. I went to the window and looked outside. Overnight the weather had gone from warm Indian summer to cold rainy fall. All the leaves had fallen and were now glistening on the ground around the naked trees. The sky was dark gray and the rain was coming down in a steady, cold sheet.

There would be no ball game today. I was glad I gave the invitation to Justin yesterday.


It rained so hard mom said we didn't have to go to church. I spent the day walking around the house looking at everything we owned to see if I could make batwings out of anything. I was so crazy with the idea that I even considered cutting up my sheet and dyeing it black. But then common sense kicked in and I realized mom would probably notice wing-shaped holes in the sheets.

By lunchtime I gave up my search and was bored out of my mind. And when I get bored I start making up games. I made up a game called, *Strange Child*. I got Danny and Bonnie to pretend like our little sister Nellie was a stranger and we didn't know who she was.

"Who's that strange child, over there?" I asked.

"I don't know, I've never seen her before," Danny added.

"I'm your *sister!*" Nellie stomped her foot.

"Sister?" Bonnie scratched her head. "But, we don't know you."

"You must be mistaken, strange child," I added. "For we have no little sister in this house."

*"Stop it!"* Nelly demanded.

Danny scowled. "Whoever that strange child is, she's kind of a brat."

"I said, *stop it!*"

I touched Nellie's hair. "Not only that, her hair is so tangled it looks like there are rats living in her head,"

"She can't possibly be our sister." Bonnie shook her head. "No one in this family has a rat's nest in her hair—"

*"I'M YOUR SISTER!"* Nelly screamed at the top of her lungs.

*"What are you kids up to?"* Dad yelled from the living room.

Sunday is dad's only day off and we're supposed to play quietly so he can have a little peace.

*"We're not doing anything!"* I yelled back. But before I could catch her and put my hand over her mouth, Nellie ran into the living room. By the time I got there, she'd ratted me out.

"Trudy, act your age. Quit tormenting your little sister," mom said, flipping through the Sunday paper.

"Why do you think it was me?"

"No one else is that nefarious."

"Good word, mom." If I compliment mom's vocabulary, she sometimes forgets what she's yelling at me about.

"Go do something quiet," dad said, picking up the sports page.

"Go read a book," mom added.

"But I've read all my books."

"Somewhere around this house there's got to be a book you haven't read," mom insisted.

"Can I read your book?"

"What book?"

"Peyton Place."

Mom got a scared look on her face. "What…where did you see that book?"

"Under the pillow on your bed—"

"Stay away from the books in my bedroom!" she said, angrily. "If you have no other books, go to grandma's house and get one. She has a whole attic full of books."

As soon as she said it, a giant light bulb went on in my brain. Not only does grandma have a whole attic full of books, she also has a whole attic full of old clothes.

And surely there would be something I could use for my bat costume.

# 15

Bonnie wanted to get a book too and even though I didn't want Bonnie to come, mom made me take her anyway.

When we got to grandma's house only grandpa was there. My grandpa is a big guy with the straightest posture you ever saw. He says that's because he grabs his elbows behind his back and forces his back straight every day. Grandpa's proud of stuff like that.

"Trudy toot-toot and Bonnie too-too!" he said when he saw as at the door. Grandpa retired from the railroad so he uses a lot of train sounds. "What are you two doing out on such a rainy day?" He opened the door and we stripped off our raincoats as we came in.

"We want to borrow some books—"

"You're in luck!" He picked up some pamphlets from the davenport. "We just got a new batch of Watch Towers—"

Grandma and grandpa are Jehovah's Witnesses and grandpa is always giving me Watch Towers pamphlets. He likes to read them 'cause they tell stories about how in heaven, *"the lion will lay down with the lamb."* Grandpa is very fond of that passage. I think it's because he doesn't like fighting and arguing. He's really looking forward to a hassle-free heaven.

"Uh, thanks grandpa…I'll take one with me. But Bonnie and I were kinda' hoping we could get some books out of the attic."

"Grandma doesn't like you kids in her attic. She's out selling Avon right now, but she'll be home soon and you can ask her then—"

"But she doesn't mind if we just get some books. We won't make a mess, I promise."

"Yeah," Bonnie added. "We won't make a mess."

Grandpa hesitated because he didn't want to get in trouble with grandma—which is one reason why he looks forward to being a lamb who can lie down with a lion. Grandma is definitely the lion of the family.

"I guess it'll be all right...but don't go digging around. Just get your books and go before grandma gets home. Okay?"

"Sure thing grandpa." But I crossed my fingers behind my back.

Grandma's attic is a museum of strange and wonderful things. Grandma has never thrown anything away in her whole life so there are old-timey clothes, books, lamps, furniture, rugs, toys and a bunch of stuff that's so old and weird I don't even know what it is.

I love the smell of grandma's attic. It's stuffy, but it's the smell of dusty discovery. I figure that's how it must smell when you go into one of those Egyptian Pyramids.

As soon as we got to the attic, Bonnie went right to the pile of books called *The Big Little Books*. They're cartoon books written for kids, but they're actually pretty interesting—not just kiddy stuff.

"Look, Trudy!" Bonnie held up a book with a bear on it. "I found an *Andy Panda!* And here's a weird one—*Perry Winkle and the Rinky Dinks*. Have you ever heard of them?"

"No," I said, my eyes darting around the room for a costume. "Must be a story about some old-timey kids."

I spotted a clothing rack with a blanket thrown over it so I made my way around a broken vacuum cleaner, a baby carriage missing a wheel, and an old typewriter that must have weighed two hundred pounds.

"Are there books over there?" Bonnie asked.

"Um...I'm checking." I lied.

I pulled the blanket off the clothes rack and sneezed as dust flew around my nose.

The rack held all kinds of clothes, so I started flipping through them. There was a blue suit with gold buttons that my grandpa wore when he worked for the railroad, a sweater vest with a big moth hole, a short woman's jacket made of scratchy brown wool...

"Trudy," Bonnie said solemnly. "We're not supposed to go digging around."

"I'm not digging. I'm just looking." I continued sliding the clothes along the rack. A green army jacket, a black polka-dot dress, a giant corset with garter snaps, a...

"But you promised grandpa you wouldn't..."

I didn't hear anything else. Behind a moth-eaten cape was the very thing I was looking for.

It was a big black skirt made of some kind of shiny material, like satin or something, and it had about a thousand pleats in it. I pulled a portion of the skirt out and it opened

71

like an accordion. What could be more perfect? I would cut the skirt in half for each wing, cut zigzags on the bottom and pin it to my sweatshirt without having to sew anything.

I could just see it—when I kept my arms down at my sides, no one would know I had wings, but when I lifted my arms all that shiny material would fan out and the zigzags would look scary and pretty and…

*"You girls better hurry!"* Grandpa yelled up the stairs. *"Grandma's gonna' be home any minute now!"*

"Okay grandpa!" I yelled down the stairs.

I took the skirt off the rack, noticing how light it was. I rolled it up to the size of small dish towel. Perfect. It would fit inside of my sweatshirt without anyone noticing…

"What are you doing?" Bonnie stared at me with a serious face.

"I'm just going to borrow this skirt."

Grandpa's voice came up the stairs. *"Girls! Grandma's in the driveway…"*

Bonnie gathered her books and stood up, then looked at me. "Are you gonna' ask grandma if you can borrow it?"

"She wont' miss it." I slid the rolled-up skirt up my sweatshirt. "I'm just going to borrow it until after Halloween, then I'll bring it back—"

72

"My Sunday school teacher said if you borrow something without asking it's the same as stealing. Are you going to steal grandma's skirt?"

"I'm not stealing it!"

"They why won't you ask grandma if you can borrow it?"

"Just keep your mouth shut about what I do! This is why I don't take you any place, Bonnie! You always stick your nose where it doesn't belong…"

*"All right girls!"* grandma's voice came up the stairs. "Come down out of my attic, *this minute!"*

*"Don't you dare tell,"* I whispered to Bonnie. Then I grabbed a Big Little Book called *Tarzan's Revenge* and headed down the stairs.

Before I got to the bottom, I turned around to threaten Bonnie one more time, but she looked so sad, the words just dried up in my mouth.

# 16

"What have I told you girls about going into my attic when I'm not home?" Grandma said when we got downstairs.

I noticed grandpa was nowhere in sight. I guess he high-tailed it out there before grandma got mad.

"We just wanted to get some books." I hugged the book to my chest so she wouldn't notice the bulge under my sweatshirt. I suddenly wished I'd taken a Zane Grey instead because the Big Little Book didn't cover very much.

"Oh, well…not much for you children to do on a rainy day. I guess it's okay if you just got some books."

Grandma set her big black Avon bag down on the dining room table and smiled. She was in such a good mood I figured she must have sold a lot of nail polish or something.

"What's the matter with you, Bonnie?" Grandma lifted Bonnie's chin to look at her. "You look like you just lost your best friend."

Bonnie raised her face, looked at grandma, then at me. She looked like she wanted to cry. "Nothing's the matter, grandma," she muttered. "I'm fine."

Okay, here's the thing.

My parents have always told me that I'm supposed to set a good example for my little sisters and brother because I'm the oldest. Most of the time I ignore my parents, 'cause it figure it's just a trick to get me to behave. But it suddenly occurred to me that maybe they were right. Maybe I did set an example and maybe the little kids would do the stuff I do, just because I'm the oldest.

I considered what Bonnie might do if she followed my example.

I could just see her growing up and meeting some guy named Clyde and the two of them running around the country robbing banks. I could see my little sister in jail, her big sad eyes staring at my parents through the bars, saying, "But I was just going to *borrow* the money…"

"What book did you get, Trudy?" Grandma asked.

"Uh…Tarzan's Revenge," I stammered. "And…and something else."

Without thinking about it, I pulled the skirt from under my sweatshirt. "I, uh, I didn't want this to get dirty so I put it under my shirt." I held the skirt up and it unrolled, revealing all the lovely pleats. "I wanted to ask if I could borrow it."

"Borrow? What for?"

"For a costume."

"Oh? Are you going to be in another school play?"

Last Christmas mom got one of grandma's old dresses and made it into a costume for my Christmas play. Since grandma was okay with that, it occurred to me that she would also be okay with my using the skirt if she thought it was for school.

"Yeah, a play…" I looked at Bonnie, and it was really weird because I swear I could see prison bars across her face. "Uh, no… I'm not going to use it for play. That is…I need it for a Halloween costume." I confessed.

"Halloween?" Grandma raised her eyebrows. "You know how I feel about Halloween."

Jehovah's Witnesses don't believe in any holiday, but they're dead set against Halloween. I don't know why. It seems to me it'd be a good holiday for them to give away their Watch Tower pamphlets to trick-or-treaters. Of course, if they did, they'd probably get their house egged.

"But grandma…it's for a party and I need a costume."

"What kind of costume?"

Okay, right here I should have *definitely* lied.

If I'd said I was going as a princess or a ballerina or anyhing like that grandma would have let me have the skirt. But there was something wrong with my mouth and the only thing that would come out was the truth.

"I'm going as a bat—"

"A cat?"

"Yeah."

I wanted to lie, I really did.

"Uh, no, not a cat… a bat."

"*A bat*—oh, I don't think so!" Grandma pushed her glasses up her nose and stared at me. "You're not going to use my nice skirt to disguise yourself as a devil creature—"

"Bats aren't devils, they're just misunderstood!"

"Don't go handing me that malarkey! I know perfectly well what bats mean on Halloween! And any girl who wants to dress up as a creature of the night needs a good talking to! I'm going to call your mother and tell her to stop letting you go to those scary movies—"

"But grandma—"

"I saw you and Paige go into the Towson Theater last month when they had that triple feature. *The House of Usher, The Bat, The Fly*—movies like that are just poison to the mind! That Vincent Price is a bad influence on kids—I've always said that, and…"

Then Grandma just went on and on and *on!*

And it made me wish I'd just gone ahead and let Bonnie become a bank robber.

# 17

**Gilbert Chemistry Set Experiment Book**

**Date:** *Tuesday, October 25, 1960*

**Experiment Objective:** *In order to make the world's most impressive bat costume I will need more moola. Objective: get more money.*

**Steps:**

**1.** *Asked dad if I could wash cars at the gas station for money. He said it was too cold and I would get sick if I got wet in this weather.*

**2.** *Called my Aunt Katie and asked if she had any work for me to do so I could earn some money. She said, no, but I could have her soda bottles to take back for the deposit.*

**3.** *Asked mom if she would take me to Towson Plaza this week so I could buy some stuff for my costume. She said, maybe.*

**Result:** *Have got original 79¢ plus whatever I get from Aunt Katie's soda bottles. Should have at least a dollar to buy material for my costume and some sequins. Since Justin is coming to the party, will definitely need sequins. Will bug mom all week until she takes me to Towson Plaza.*

After school, I got off the school bus, ran home and changed into my jeans. It was cold but sunny, so I figured I better return the pop bottles before it rained again. Besides, it was Tuesday, the day Paige and I always walk to the store.

I didn't discuss that plan with Paige because her mom picked her up after school so I didn't see her on the bus. But it was our usual day to walk to the store, so I headed out.

I grabbed my wagon and took off down the street. My Aunt Katie's house is three houses past Paige's, but even so, I had to get the pop bottles first.

When I got to Aunt Katie's house I was overjoyed to find she had a whole case of bottles for me. Aunt Katie said she got her neighbors to contribute so my trip to the store would be worthwhile. This is why my Aunt Katie is my best buddy. She's always doing neat things that you don't expect a grown-up to do.

I rolled my wagon full of bottles to Paige's house. Although we usually buy candy with the money, today I was going to save it for my costume. I didn't think Paige would mind because she gets an allowance every week and can buy candy without using pop bottle money.

I got to her house and I knocked on the door. Paige's mom wasn't home so I expected Paige to answer, but a strange girl opened the door. Her blonde hair was curled and neat with a blue velvet ribbon holding the curls. The ribbon matched her sweater and she had a lace collar coming out of the top. Her skirt was pleated blue plaid and she wore knee-high socks and loafers with pennies in them. She looked like one of those girls in the Breck shampoo ads.

"Hi," she said, looking me up and down.

I was wearing my old jeans with holes in the knees and my red sweatshirt. It was kind of cold, so I had the hood pulled up, and when I pulled it down the static electricity made my hair get all *Bride of Frankenstein*, so she must have thought I was weird. Then she looked at my wagon and said, "Are you collecting bottles or something?"

"Uh…no. I mean, yes…I mean, is Paige here?"

"Yes…," she turned and yelled up the stairs. *"Paige! Some girl with a wagon is here to see you!"*

*"Oh, that's Trudy!"* Paige yelled down the stairs. "Tell her to come in, I'll be down in a minute."

The strange girl opened the door for me, but she gave me one of *those* looks. It was the kind of look Paige's mom gives me when she thinks I can't see her.

"You can leave your wagon outside," the strange girl said. "I don't think anyone will steal your pop bottles."

*"Well, duh!"* There was something about this girl I didn't like. "Like I'd bring a wagon in the house…"

"I didn't mean to insult you." The girl gave me a phony smile. "It's just that I don't know you, so I wasn't sure what you'd do." She stepped away so I could come in.

I didn't like the way this girl was taking over Paige's house like she owned it.

"By the way, my name's Cassandra," she said. "I'm Paige's friend."

Okay, now I know why I didn't like her. This was the girl who was, not only trying to take over our Halloween party, but also trying to take over Paige.

"And I'm Trudy," I said, adding, "I'm Paige's *real* friend—"

Just then Paige came bounding down the stairs. I was surprised to see she was still in her school clothes. By now Paige was usually in her jeans, but instead, she was wearing an outfit that looked like Cassandra's. And I wondered if they planned it that way.

"Oh, good," Paige said. "You met Cassandra! Mom picked us up after school so we could plan the Halloween party." Then she looked away from me, like she was afraid I was going to blow my top or something.

"And what have you been *planning?*" I asked Paige, but the creepy girl answered instead.

"Well… like I was telling Paige…the decorations you two bought are *okay*, but I really wish you'd spent more money on the contest prizes."

"We spent almost $4 on the records and the prizes," I said indignantly.

"But the prizes aren't exactly top notch, now are they?"

"What does that mean?"

"It means you should have gotten stuff like fingernail polish, lipstick and jewelry for the girls, and pen knifes, soap-on-a-rope and little bottles of Old Spice for the boys. Those would have been *good* prizes. But instead you bought stuff like yo-yo's and bubble-blow and—"

"I'd love to get any of those prizes!"

"I'm sure you would," she said in a snooty way. "But junior high kids expect a little more. I mean, how am I supposed to talk this party up to everyone if I can't mention what kind of cool stuff they'll get if they come?"

"You mean you have to *bribe* kids to come to the party?"

"Well, sort of." She picked a piece of lint off her sweater. "I mean, Paige is younger than everyone else in our class and they might not want to come if they think it's a little kid's party. But if I tell them about all the cool prizes, they'll understand that it's a party for older kids—not babies."

I expected Paige to get mad about being called a baby, but instead she said, "See, Trudy? This is why I need Cassandra to help with the party. I would have never thought about stuff like that."

"Which is why we need to get better prizes," Cassandra said. "Can you get your mom to give you more money?"

"She already gave me a ten-dollar bill and I never gave her any change. I don't think she'll give me any more…"

"That's okay, I've got a plan—but we'll talk about that later." Cassandra turned her back to me, adding, *"When we're alone."* Then Cassandra turned around with a sneaky look on her face, and I wondered what she was up to.

"Oh, by the way," she said speaking to me. "Paige tells me you're inviting someone to the party. Does your friend know this isn't a little kid party? I mean, I wouldn't want you to bring someone who's going to feel, well,…you know,…*out of place."*

"Out of place? Oh, I suppose that's possible." To force the smile from my face, I looked at my fingernails like there was something really important there. "Because, you see, Cassandra, he's in *high school* and he might think junior high kids are a little young for him." I bit my cheek to keep from laughing at her.

Cassandra looked kinda' mad. Then she acted like she didn't believe me. *"Really?* Well, what school does he go to?"

"He goes to Loyola High."

"I see…a *Catholic* school."

She said it in such strange way, I couldn't figure out what she was getting at. But Paige ignored her and said, "Trudy...you invited a *boy?*"

"Of course." I acted all nonchalant like I invite boys to parties all the time.

"Where do you know him from?"

"Oh...we play baseball together and look at the stars at night...you know, stuff like that."

Paige looked like she was really impressed. "Wow, Trudy, I never knew."

Paige wasn't allowed to play baseball with the rest of the neighborhood because one time a ball jammed her finger and the knuckle swelled up really bad. After that Mrs. H. wouldn't let Paige play ball because she didn't want Paige to get deformed. And because of that, Paige never met Justin and she didn't know that when I sat under the stars with him, it was with ten other kids.

"Well, girls, this has been lovely." I imitated my mother when she wants to leave the room. I walked to the door saying, " I'd love to stay and chat, but I have to get to the store before it gets dark."

I held the door open for a minute, then turned and said, "Oh, by the way, *Cassandra?"*

She had her arms crossed and looked like she didn't want to answer me, but she did anyway. "Yes, Trudy?"

"See that you get some prizes *high school* boys would like…*okay?*"

Then I closed the door before she could answer.

# 18

The next morning I talked mom into taking me to Towson Plaza after school so I could get material for my costume. I could probably get her to sew it too, if I could convince her that her reputation as a housekeeper would be seriously damaged if Mrs. H. saw me in a poorly sewn costume. Yeah, that'll work.

At school, my teacher Mr. Harmon was reading us a poem. Mr. Harmon used to teach at the elementary school, but he switched to Towsontown the same year I did. I never had Mr. Harmon in elementary, but I knew him because he directed all the school plays. And, last year when I was in the Christmas play, I did something that could have gotten me expelled, but Mr. Harmon jumped in and saved my bacon. Ever since then he's been my hero.

Today he was giving us a lesson on *literature metaphors*—which is when someone says one thing, but it means something else. He was reading the class a poem by a guy named Wordsworth. He said the poem was about *vanishing youth*—which means the guy was getting old and not happy about it. I figured ol' Wordsworth must have found a gray hair before he wrote it, 'cause my mom gets all weird like that when she finds one.

Because Mr. Harmon is a play director, when he reads something he makes it come alive. He was reading the end of the poem saying:

>...though nothing can bring back the hour
>Of splendor in the grass,
>Of glory in the flower,
>We will grieve not, but rather find...

He was interrupted by a knock on the classroom door. It was Mary, a girl I sit with at lunch who's also a hallway monitor.

"Mr. Harmon? It's time for the girls to go to the nurse's office." When she saw me, she twiddled her fingers in *hello.*

"Thank you, Mary. I nearly forgot." He closed his poetry book and stood up. "Okay, I want just the girls to line up and follow Mary to the nurse's office—"

"Why just them?" one of the boys asked.

"Because they're having a special lesson that only concerns girls," Mr. Harmon answered. "But don't worry, guys, you're in luck; we get to stay here and read more poetry…"

All the guys moaned, and that made Mr. Harmon laugh, so I knew they weren't going to read poetry.

As we walked to the nurse's office, I whispered to Mary, "What's going on?" But she just put her finger to her lips and whispered, "No talking in the hallways." I hate when someone's job goes to their head.

We got to the nurse's office and it was filled with chairs, so we all took a seat and waited. After a while, Miss Jenkins, the Phys Ed teacher walked in and stood at the head of the room.

"Hello girls," she said as she shoved a Kleenex up her nose and swirled it around. Pulling it out, she stared at the tissue for a minute, then stuck it in her pocket.

Ignoring the fact that she'd just pocketed a booger, Miss Jenkins continued. "Usually Nurse Gail gives this lesson, but she's out sick today, so I'm going to be your teacher."

I had to bite my lip to keep from moaning. I don't like Miss Jenkins and she doesn't like me. But she's quite evil, so

I knew better than to make any noise 'cause that would only give her an excuse to give me detention.

Miss Jenkins passed out pamphlets, saying, "Each of you take one and pass the rest to the person behind you." When I got mine, I read the cover, *Now, You're a Young Lady!* which gave me no clue why we were in the nurse's office.

After the pamphlets were distributed, Miss Jenkins went to the front of the room and pulled down a rolled up chart that had a picture of a gut shaped like a triangle. Then she started talking, using words like *Uterus, Fallopian,* and *Ovaries.* She talked about unfertilized eggs and monthly flows, but I still didn't know what she was talking about.

I flipped through the pamphlet trying to figure it out, but there were no answers there either. I read how, "*a girl should stand straight with her chin up and sit with good posture so there will be room for her organs to function properly...*" But I still didn't know what they were talking about. And that really worried me 'cause it was like that Vincent Price movie, *The Tingler* where everyone has a parasite inside them and it kills you if you get too scared. What was this pamphlet trying to tell me?

And there was more weird stuff about something called *menstruation* and how it made you have uncontrollable moods—like anger or sadness—and that made me think of that other movie, *Invasion of the Body Snatchers*, where space aliens took over people's lives and they acted all weird and stuff.

Then there were pictures of strange contraptions called *pin-less belts with adjustable clasps,* and *sanitary napkins.* And it made me wonder if this pamphlet was trying to tell humans to protect themselves against the menstruation invaders by using that stuff. But it didn't explain how.

But what really bothered me was a picture of an old-fashioned lady in a big dress with a parasol, and under the picture it said, *"She didn't know about Kotex."* And that really scared me because I didn't know about Kotex either. So, I flipped through the book, desperately trying to find out what happened to her, but it didn't say. And that made me feel totally unprotected. Did the menstruation take over her mind and body and make her a zombie or something?

The class was nearly over, and I still didn't understand any of this gut-stuff. I was really scared that I would end up like the old-fashioned lady who didn't know about Kotex, so I raised my hand.

"Yes, Trudy?" Miss Jenkins said in a mean way, like I was asking a question just to bug her.

"I still don't understand what this is about..."

"Well, it's not my fault if you weren't listening..."

"But, I don't understand either," another girl said, then another one said the same thing and Miss Jenkins got all mad and barked, "If you don't understand, then go home and ask your mothers! It's not my job to spell it out for you!"

Then she snapped the picture of the gut closed and said, "Now, everyone line up and get back to your classroom."

The whole way back to class, that poem Mr. Harmon was reading kept playing over and over in my brain. *"...though nothing can bring back the hour, of splendor in the grass, of glory in the flower..."*

And I wondered how that dumb poem ended.

# 19

At the end of the day, as the school bus pulled up to my dad's gas station, I looked out the window and saw Paige. Since she wasn't on the bus, I figured her mom must have picked her up and brought her home again, which was something her mom had been doing a lot lately.

Because Paige was waiting for me, I figured she must have something important to tell me. I was hoping she'd say Cassandra couldn't come to the party because she'd been kidnapped by Martians or run over by a Good Humor truck.

When the bus stopped, all the kids jumped off the steps and ran away, like if they didn't hurry, the bus would drag them back to school.

Paige was still in her school clothes so I figured she must have just gotten home and hurried down the street to catch me. "Hey, Paige," I smiled. "What's new?"

But she just crossed her arms and jutted her chin out like she was mad about something. "Trudy...I have to ask you something."

"Okay."

"That boy you asked to my party..."

"Yeah?"

"Is he Catholic?"

"I think so. Why?"

"So...you invited a *Catholic boy* to my party without asking me first?"

I didn't know what she was getting at. "Yeah...I guess I did."

Paige seemed to get even madder. "Well, now you're just going to have to *un-invite* him." She put her hands on her hips and made a face like she was waiting for me to argue with her.

I thought she was joking so I smiled and waited for her to laugh. But when she didn't, I got confused. "You want me to un-invite Justin? But why?"

"Because he's *Catholic,* that's why!" She re-crossed her arms.

I couldn't understand her anger or why she didn't want Justin at the party. It was so weird I didn't even have room in my brain to get upset.

"What does being Catholic have to do with anything?"

"It's got to do with a lot of things!" Paige insisted. But her eyes were racing around like she was trying to think of something.

"Tell me one thing that's wrong with Catholic boys." The strangeness was starting to wear off and I was beginning to get a little mad.

"Well, for one thing—they wear those weird crosses!"

"What?"

"You know how *we* wear plain crosses? Well, Catholics wear crosses with a big bloody Jesus hanging on it." Then she got all huffy and said, *"How gross!"*

"But I've never seen Justin wear a bloody Jesus…"

"He probably wears it under his shirt!" Then she talked to me like I was a little kid. "I mean, how would it look if he showed up at my party wearing a bloody Jesus around his neck?"

"But he's coming as Dracula—"

*"That's even worse!* He'll be dressed as Dracula with a bloody Jesus around his neck and it'll look like he sucked the blood out of our savior! And that's just plain …*unholy!"*

"What?"

"Cassandra was right!" Paige threw her hands up in the air, like she was sorry she didn't listen to her sooner.

"Cassandra said a boy with his Catholic cooties would only cause problems and—"

Okay, now it made sense.

Paige had never said anything about Catholics before. I mean, *for crying out loud,* she even owned a nun doll! And I might not know much about religions but I was pretty sure nuns were Catholic and I bet that ol' nun doll on Paige's bookshelf had a big bloody Jesus around her neck—so what difference did it make? None of that junk bothered her before Cassandra put all that weird stuff in her brain. And just thinking about Cassandra made me so mad I could have spit nickels.

"...and Cassandra said if I let a Catholic come to the party, then I might as well invite an immigrant kid to bring some of their stinky steamed cabbage—"

"The only bad smell around here is Cassandra!" I yelled. "She's just a big, fat, stinky creep!"

"No, she's not!"

"She thinks she's hot snot on a silver platter, but she's really just a cold booger on a paper plate—"

"You're the cold booger, *Trudy!*"

"No, *you* are!"

"If I'm such a cold booger, well, then... *maybe you shouldn't come to my party!*"

I was stunned.

Paige and I had planned this party since we were in the second grade. We spent four years planning the perfect Halloween party, and now she was kicking me out? That really hurt.

But I was darned if I'd let her know.

*"So what?* Who wants to come to a dumb ol' party with a germ like Cassandra, anyway? With her there it's just going to be one big, fat, *booger ball!*

*"Oh, yeah?* Well, Cassandra doesn't like you either—and neither does my mother! Mom said you're just a bad influence and I shouldn't associate with you—and maybe she's right. Maybe I *should* get some new friends..."

Okay, here's the thing, I always knew Paige's mother didn't like me, but Paige and I never talked about it, so I could always pretend it wasn't true. But hearing Paige say it out loud made it real. And impossible to ignore.

I was still trying to act like she didn't hurt me. "Since when do you care what your mother says?"

"Since *now,* that's when!"

My wounded feelings suddenly turned to anger and I wanted to hurt Paige as much as she hurt me. So, I put my hand on my hip and flapped my other hand around like it was made of rubber. *"Oh, look at me!* I'm Paige's mother and I don't like Trudy—oh, wait a minute—let me drink some sparkling burgundy…" I went *glug, glug, glug,* then wiped my mouth and staggered around, saying, "Oh, that's better! Now I like *EVERYBODY!*"

"You shut up about my mother!"

"You make me!"

Paige balled her fists and came closer, and I did the same. It was beginning to look like a fight was unavoidable, when suddenly my grandmother's voice pierced the air around us.

*"All right you girls! There will be no fighting!"*

I looked around, but couldn't see her.

That's the thing about my grandma; she could have been at a window, behind a tree or on the porch. You never knew where she was or how she knew what was going on. Grandma was like *The Phantom.*

"Where is she?" Paige whispered, looking around.

"I don't know…"

*"Young ladies do not fight!"* Grandma yelled. *"Now, you two get home…"*

Paige shook her fist at me. "Lucky for you…"

I shook my fist back at her. "No, *you're* the lucky one…"

*"DID YOU HEAR ME? I SAID NO FIGHTING!"*

And we both walked away as quiet as cotton balls.

# 20

I did what I always do when I'm upset. I ran to the apple tree in my grandpa's garden. I threw my schoolbooks on the ground and started climbing. I still had on my school clothes, but I didn't care. I didn't care that I was wearing a skirt and anyone who came into the garden could look up and see my underpants. And I didn't care if grandma saw me, either. If she yelled for me to get down, I'd just pretend like I didn't hear her.

When I got to the very top I wedged my butt between two branches and took a long time looking around. From the top of the tree I could see the pumpkin patch with spots of orange among the dying vines. Grandpa had already harvested the corn, so the corn stalks were all batched together like teepees. Off in the distance, someone was burning leaves and I could see the smoke rising up to the sky.

Everything looked cold and dying, the grass, the leaves, the corn, even the earth looked old and lonely. Usually I like this kind of weather because it's spooky and Halloween-y, but today it just made me sad.

It was cloudy and the sky was dark gray. The wind picked up, blowing cold air up my skirt and it made me shiver. In the distance some kids were playing, but I didn't feel any happiness watching them. They just looked like bugs.

The reason I climb trees when I'm upset is because I get to see the world in miniature and sometimes it makes my problems look small too. But today I was too numb to even think about my problems. All I could do was hurt.

I hurt because I used to be Paige's best friend, but now Cassandra was her best friend. I hurt because I'd have to tell Justin that we'd both been un-invited to the party. I hurt because all my plans for being the world's scariest bat were now spoiled. And I hurt because next year I'd be too old to go trick-or-treating and I wanted this to be the last great Halloween, the kind I would remember my whole life.

But now it was going to be the worst.

After a while I got cold and climbed down the tree. But when I jumped off the lower branch, I landed on a rotten apple and got brown goo all over my school shoes. And that made me even sadder because the squashed apple was like my heart, all mashed up and spoiled.

I wiped my shoe off in the dead leaves, picked up my schoolbooks and went down the driveway to my house. When I opened the door, mom was standing there with her car keys in her hand.

"All right!" she said all happy and excited. "Who wants to go to Towson Plaza for some Halloween shopping?"

And I did something I haven't done since I was a little kid.

I burst out crying.

## 21

Mom sent all the kids outside to play then she took me to her bedroom and sat me on the bed.

"Okay, Trudy," she said, in a nice voice. "Now, what's the matter?"

I told her everything.

I was so upset I didn't even try to change the facts or hide anything. I told her about the party, about Cassandra and her cootie-catchers, about inviting Justin, and how Paige uninvited me because Justin was Catholic. Then I told her how Mrs. H. didn't like me and said that I was a bad influence on Paige. Mom looked kind of mad when I told her that, but when I told her about imitating Mrs. H. drinking sparkling burgundy, mom had to turn her head so I wouldn't see her smile.

"You shouldn't have done that," she said, trying to hide her grin. "But that Patricia Haussman does put on airs. She thinks she's so sophisticated because she buys wine by the case. But that only means that she drinks it by the..." Mom suddenly stopped talking. "Well...never mind about that."

"Is there something wrong with Catholics?" I asked because I really wasn't sure.

Mom shook her head like she does when she's disgusted about something. "There's nothing wrong with Catholics, Trudy. That stuff is just in that girl's mind."

"But how am I going to tell Justin that he can't come to the party?"

Mom thought about it for a minute. "You're not going to un-invite him."

"But mom…"

"You're going to tell him the party's been moved to your house."

"What?"

"We'll straighten up the basement and have the party here. You can invite everyone in the neighborhood— everyone that Paige snubbed."

Our basement was nothing like Paige's rec room. She had wall-to-wall carpet and wood paneled walls and nice furniture. Our basement was just cement floors and cinderblock walls with bare poles holding up the ceiling. Mom's washer and dryer are in the basement and so is a big old furnace with silver ductwork coming out of it like the arms of a giant robot. There's nothing pretty about our basement.

"But we don't have any Halloween decorations—"

"*Sure we do!* We'll go to grandpa's garden and get a bunch of pumpkins and carve them into jack-o-lanterns. We'll put candles in them and set them around the room and it'll be all spooky and Halloween-y! *Oh!* And we can bring some cornstalks from the garden and set them against the walls and grandpa can give you some dried ears of corn and—"

"But what about refreshments—won't that cost a lot of money?"

It was October and that meant mom and dad were scrimping and saving so they could order a tank of fuel oil for the furnace. Our tank was nearly empty and it would cost $60 to fill it so our house could stay warm all winter. I knew mom didn't have any money to spare.

"We'll make do. You get a basket of apples from grandpa's tree and I'll buy a big bag of sugar to make some candy apples. I'll buy some packs of Kool aid for drinks, and I'll make some sugar cookies, and maybe buy a bag of candy corn—that won't cost too much. It might not be a feast at the Taj Mahal, but I think everyone will enjoy it."

Next to the elaborate party Paige and I had planned this sounded pretty poor.

I mean, I could just imagine Justin coming into our dark, dusty basement with a bunch of moldy cornstalks thrown against the wall and some ol' pumpkins rotting on the floor. We didn't even have a table down there, so where would we put the refreshments? I could just see mom setting a pitcher of Kool Aid and a bowl of candy corn on the dryer, saying, *"Come and get it!"*

But I didn't want to hurt mom's feelings by telling her any of that stuff.

"I don't know, mom. It seems like an awful lot of work...for you, I mean."

"Oh, don't be silly!" she said all happy and peppy. "It'll be fun!"

"Yeah, but I don't really—"

She looked at the clock next to the bed and jumped up. *"Oh, my gosh!* Look at the time! I need to get to the A&P and get something for dinner! We won't have time to buy your material today, but I promise I'll take you tomorrow. Now, you watch your little sisters and brother while I dash to the store. Okay?"

I didn't want the party, but I didn't know how to tell her. "Uh...sure. I'll watch them."

I figured, what the heck? I could always tell mom later.

# 22

Mom came home from the A&P with two bags of groceries. As she unpacked everything she held up a can of Hershey's cocoa powder for me to see.

"Look, Trudy! Look what I got!"

"Yeah…"

"You know what that means, don't you?

"Uh…no."

"Okay," she said, pulling a ten-pound bag of sugar out the bag. "Now do you know what it means?"

"Still, no."

"Silly! It means I can make fudge for your party!"

"Fudge?" Danny said. "Fudge for a party?"

"Yay, party!" Nellie clapped her hands.

"Party?" Bonnie said. "What party?"

"Trudy is having a Halloween party in our basement!"

"Can we come?" Bonnie asked.

"Of course you can!" Mom pulled more stuff out of the bags. "The whole neighborhood can come!"

"Can Anna come?" Bonnie asked.

"Can Leroy come?" Danny added.

"Everyone can come!" mom said, all happy and excited.

"Can Howdy Doody come?" Nellie asked.

"Sure he can! And Clara Belle too!" Mom pulled Kool Aid packets out of the bag. "Look Trudy—I got cherry and lemon, red and yellow—so when I mix them together they'll turn orange and we'll tell everyone it's pumpkin juice—won't that be fun?"

"Why didn't you just buy the orange flavor?

"Oh...I didn't think of that."

But it wasn't the Kool Aid I was paying attention to, it was the other stuff mom was pulling out of the bag—the stuff she bought for dinner. She pulled out a package of baloney and a can of baked beans. That meant she was going to make baloney bowls—which was fried baloney that curled up into a bowl and she filled the bowl with baked beans.

Now, all us kids love baloney bowls, but dad hates it—he calls them *baloney bowels*. And the only time mom makes them is when she doesn't have money to buy regular food.

I looked at the Hershey's powder, the ten-pound bag of sugar and the Kool Aid and I figured mom spent all her food money on stuff for my party.

A party I didn't want.

# 23

Dad came home and when he saw what mom had on the table for dinner he got all huffy. "Baloney *bowels?*" he griped. "I thought you had $3 to buy food, so why are we eating baloney?"

"We'll talk about it later, Dale." Mom gave him *that look,* the one parents give each other when they don't want to discuss something in front of the kids.

"We're gonna' have a party!" Nelly told dad as she danced around his legs.

"What party?"

"A Halloween party! And Howdy Doody is coming!"

Dad looked at mom, waiting for an answer, but she just ignored him and filled the baloney bowls with baked beans. "Thelma?"

"We'll talk later, Dale."

After dinner mom sent me to the basement to move the storage boxes under the stairs so they wouldn't be in the way.

Our basement is kind of creepy. There's only one light bulb in the ceiling and it makes weird shadows on the wall as you move around. I moved the boxes of summer clothes under the stairs. Then I took a broom and started sweeping the dust from the cement floors.

As I swept, I planned how I was going to tell mom that I didn't want the party. I practiced different ways of saying it, trying to figure out the best way. *I don't want dad to get mad at you, I don't want you to have to work so hard, It's too much trouble, It's...*

Suddenly there was a loud, *WHOOSH,* and a yellow light began flickering on the wall near the dryer. The first thing I thought was *GHOST* and I dropped the broom to run upstairs. But before I hit the first stair, I realized it was just the furnace kicking on. When the furnace goes on, flames whoosh up inside it, and light from the flames comes out a little hole and dances on the wall nearby. The furnace hadn't been turned on all summer, so I forgot about the ghostly flickering.

I was just starting to relax when mom came down the stairs. "Good job, Trudy! You got all the boxes moved!"

"Yeah, but I was thinking—we really don't have a table for the refreshments, so maybe we shouldn't have—"

"Of course, we have a table!" She went to the storage side of the basement and pulled out two of dad's sawhorses.

"We'll set these up over there and put that old door on top of them and *voilá!* a table! Neat, huh?"

The table looked crappy, but mom looked so proud of her creation, I didn't want to hurt her feelings. "Yeah, mom, neat..."

I figured I better tell her right away. "You know mom, I was thinking, maybe this party isn't such a good—"

"Oh, by the way, I called Justin's mother and told her the party was moved to our house."

"You what?"

"I had to call her anyway—we're both on the Lady's Auxiliary for the fire department. So while we were discussing the fundraiser, I told her to tell Justin the party was now going to be at our house..."

I felt like I did last summer when I went to Ocean City and got in the ocean for the first time. Out of nowhere a big wave came along and, with a loud roar, it picked me up and pushed me halfway down the beach. The wave was so powerful that no matter how much kicking and paddling I did, I couldn't go anywhere except where the wave wanted me to go.

Mom stopped for a minute and looked around the basement. "You know Trudy, I never realized it before, but this room is perfect for a party! Don't you think?"

I looked around the room and wondered what she was seeing. The only thing I could see was dust, cement walls, weird shadows, and…

*WHOOSH!*

I knew what it was, but I jumped anyway because the furnace sounded just like that wave at Ocean City.

# 24

When we finished with the basement, mom told me to call Miriam Langston and invite her to the party. Mom never lets us kids use the phone because we have a party-line—which means we share our telephone service with another family—and mom thinks it's rude for kids to hog the line when adults have important things to talk about; like sharing recipes, gossiping, and stuff like that.

"But why do I have to call her?"

"Because you want to give her time to make plans. Tomorrow you can go to the bus stop early and invite the neighborhood kids who go to Elementary school."

"But not all of them," I insisted.

"Why not?"

"Well…I'm not going to invite the Smellys."

"Don't call them that, their name is *Smellie*—and, *yes,* you will also invite Melvin and Jacob."

"But, *mom…*"

113

"You're not going to hurt their feelings by snubbing them. You don't want to act like…," Mom glanced at Nellie who was hanging on every word. Nellie is like a little parrot that goes around repeating everything, so you have to be careful what you say.

Mom nodded at Nellie, reminding me to watch what I said. "You don't want to act like *you know who*. Anyway, I want you to call Miriam and invite her so she can start working on her costume."

Oh, great.

Not only will the party be in our dusty, dark basement but the Smellys will be there and so will Miriam Langston.

Miriam and I used to be worst enemies. But last year I locked her in our dark basement and when she came out she tried to beat the crap out of me. But mom caught her and Miriam got in big trouble. Ever since then we've been friendly to each other. I don't know how it happened, but it did. And since we're not enemies anymore I didn't mind inviting her to the party, except for one little thing.

Miriam isn't much on baseball, but she comes to our games anyway because Justin is there. After the game, while everyone's sitting on the grass looking at the stars, Miriam rolls onto her stomach, puts her face in her hands and stares at Justin like he's one of the stars. And if that isn't bad enough, she kind of wiggles her rear end while she's doing it. And that really bugs me because sometimes Justin watches her.

But Mom made me invite her anyway.

I guess it will be okay. I didn't think Miriam would get the chance to roll on her stomach and stare at Justin. And even if she did, I could always tell her to stop. After all, it was *my* party and *my* basement, so I'd be the boss.

"You heard me, Miriam," I'd say in a stern voice. "Get off your stomach *right now!* I don't know what kind of parties you're used to going to, but at *this* party we will have no butt-wiggling!"

Let her try that stuff at my party and I'd tell her off, but good.

# 25

The elementary school bus picks up kids before the Junior High bus does, so I had to go to the bus stop early to invite the neighborhood kids to the Halloween party. It was Thursday and the party was only two days away, but no one minded the last minute invitation. Everyone was just happy to be invited to a Halloween party. Even the Smelly brothers.

At first, Melvin and Jacob were suspicious of the invitation, but when it finally sunk in that I wasn't kidding them, the Smelly boys got all smiley and dopey-looking.

They got on the bus, and as I walked away, I saw the Smellys stare at me from the bus window. When I looked up, they both grinned at me like a couple of goofs. I figured it must have been the first time anyone ever invited them to a party. I only hoped those two idiots wouldn't get a crush on me.

After school, mom took me to S.S. Kresge's at Towson Plaza, and she did something she's never done before—she let me go shopping by myself. Usually mom doesn't let me out of her sight, but she said I was old enough to go on my own, so she went to look at housewares while I went downstairs to find material for my costume.

Since it was going to be crappy party, I figured I should at least salvage my idea about being the world's coolest bat. Then maybe Justin would be too busy staring at me to notice a party with a washer and dryer in the middle of it. Or Miram's butt.

I had almost $2 to spend, which was enough to buy fancy material, a couple packs of sequins and some plastic fangs. I planned to buy silver sequins so it would look like moonlight bouncing off the batwings. And that was such a cool idea it made me want to write a poem about it.

I took a hand basket from the front of the store and headed to the back. On the way, I passed the Halloween decorations and just seeing the orange and black crepe paper made me sad. I thought of all the years Paige and I planned our perfect party and how much fun we had picking out all the Halloween stuff last weekend.

My party wasn't going to have decorations or contest prizes. My party wouldn't be in a carpeted, wood-paneled rec room, but would be in a dark, unfinished basement. And just when I was really starting to feel sorry for myself, someone said, "Trudy? Is that you?"

I turned around and was face to face with Cassandra.

She was with another girl who was dressed almost identically—both of them wearing the same color sweaters, knee-highs and hair ribbons. The only difference was, one wore a plaid skirt and the other wore a plain skirt. Did Cassandra call these girls up every night and tell them what to wear?

"I thought that was you, Trudy," she said, grinning like an ear of corn. "I was sorry to hear you won't be coming to our Halloween party." Then she elbowed the girl next to her.

I forced myself to stay cool. I didn't want Cassandra to know how hurt I was. "Well, you see…I'm having my own party, and—"

"Oh, yes, I heard." Cassandra turned to her friend and they both suppressed a giggle.

Mom only decided about the party yesterday, and already Cassandra-the-Terrible knew? "How did you find out?"

"Miriam Langston told me. I think she was upset that we didn't invite her to the *good* party so she bragged about being invited to your little thing."

The creepy girl with Cassandra, said, "Can you believe it? She actually *bragged* about it—like it was something special!"

Cassandra turned to the girl and they started talking to each other like I was invisible.

"I know, *right?*"

"She even bragged about her costume!"

"A queen costume! Can you imagine?"

"Sure I can—*queen of the cooties!*"

They both started laughing until an older girl came around the corner and said, "Let's go! I need to get home before the Buddy Deane show comes on."

"You're sister's so bossy," the mean girl whispered.

"I know, *right?*"

And they both walked away from me like I wasn't even there.

# 26

There are a hundred things I hate about Cassandra, not the least of which was the way she kept saying *our party*, like she owned Paige.

It just wasn't right.

Paige and I spent years planning that party, and I spent all day helping her pick out the decorations. But now it's Cassandra's party? What right did she have to say that? It just wasn't fair.

I thought about Paige's rec room all decorated for Halloween. She'd have a paper tablecloth with Halloween stuff printed on it, matching napkins and a witch centerpiece that folded out like an accordion. Hanging on the wall behind the table would be skeletons and black cats with moveable arms and legs. And most important of all—orange and black crepe paper streamers twisted and hung up all around the room.

And what would I have?

An old door on two sawhorses and ugly cinderblock walls.

And *NO* orange and black crepe paper streamers.

But even with none of that stuff, Miriam still bragged to Cassandra that she was coming to my party. I remembered Paige telling me how Miriam got picked on, pushed into the boys' lavatory and stuff like that. So I thought it was brave of Miriam to brag to that stinky ol' +-Cassandra that she was going to another party—even one as plain as mine. So what if Cassandra and her evil friend made fun of her? I was still proud of Miriam.

And what about my mom? She made dad eat baloney so she'd have enough money to buy stuff for the party. That was unselfish, *and* brave.

Then I thought about the all the kids at the bus stop and how excited they were that I was throwing a party. Even the Smelly brothers were over-the-moon happy. In fact, the Smellys almost seemed *touched.* And I guess that was kind of brave of them to show everyone that they had feelings, because if they weren't careful we might expect them to act like human beings *all* the time.

Everyone was happy about my party.

Everyone was acting brave and unselfish.

Everyone—that is—except me.


I looked at my empty hand basket.

Then I looked at the orange and black crepe paper.

# 27

Danny, Bonnie and Nellie wanted to help me decorate, but since I spent my own money on the decorations, I got to be the boss and said, *No!* Nellie started to pitch a fit but mom told her to cut it out. Mom told her she'd be surprised on Saturday when she got to see the basement all decorated for Halloween.

The first thing I did was wrap orange and black crepe paper around the bare poles that held up the ceiling, then I hung some of it from the stairs—because crept paper streamers are a *must* for any party.

Then I put the Halloween tablecloth over the old door on the sawhorses and it looked like a real table. I couldn't afford the skeletons and black cats, but I got some colored construction paper and my mom (who's a pretty good artist) cut out cats and pumpkins to hang on the walls. She even made a purple witch, which was kinda' neat.

Although I only had two dollars, I still managed to buy a few prizes for the contests. I got two pairs of wax lips because they were only a nickel each, and the rest of the prizes I got from the penny gumball machine. I got gumballs of course, but I also got some of the prizes that come in those little plastic bubbles—like a tiny glow-in-the-dark skull, which I wanted to keep for myself, but didn't. I figured I would put it all in a grab bag and the prizewinners would close their eyes to grab a prize.

And there was one thing I bought that I knew Paige wouldn't have at her party.

A rubber bat.

I hung the bat from the ceiling over the table. It was on a rubber cord and flapped its wings when you pulled on it. I purposely hung it high enough so the Smelly boys couldn't pull it down, 'cause that's the kind of stuff they like to do.

When I was done I looked around the room. It wasn't perfect, but at least it looked more like a party than a dingy basement.

I'd made headway on something.

But not on everything.

I still didn't have a costume, and now I had no money to buy material. Today was Thursday and I only had two more days to get a costume. I didn't know what I was going to do, so I just pulled on the rubber bat and watched it go up and down.

"Take *that* Paige Haussman!" I said as I watched the bat flap its wings. "You're not gonna' have one of these babies at your dumb party!"

*"Trudy!"* mom yelled from upstairs. "Paige is on the phone and she wants to talk to you!"

Whoa, that was strange.

Was it a coincidence, or did she hear me?

# 28

On my way up the stairs, I wondered why Paige was calling. Was she sorry for everything she said to me? Did she want to apologize? Did she still want to be friends?

Or—best of all—was she going to tell me Cassandra was squashed by a sputnik?

By the time I got to the phone, I was pretty much convinced that one of those things was true, so when I answered, I used a real cheery voice. "Hello, Paige! What's new—"

But Paige didn't answer back in a cheery voice. "Is it true you're having a Halloween party on the same night as me?"

"Yeah..."

"You're a big copycat—"

"You don't *own* Halloween! And what difference does it make to you? I'm not inviting any of *your* creepy friends—"

"No, but you're inviting the Smellys."

"So? *You* didn't invite them."

*"And with good reason!* When they asked if I was going to your party, I said, *Heck no!* I told them that I wouldn't come to any germy party given by Trudy McFarlan, and do you know what they said?"

I didn't know but I could sure imagine.

"They said on the night of my party they're going to hide in the bushes by my house. And when my friends show up they're *going to throw rotten eggs at them!"*

That struck me as really funny because I could just see ol' Cassandra with egg dripping off her velvet hair ribbon into her snooty face. I guess I must have chuckled because Paige got even madder.

*"It's not funny, Trudy!"*

I suddenly got fed up with the whole thing. "I don't understand you anymore, Paige. I mean, you used to think throwing eggs at people was funny! Now you're like some persnickety old lady—"

"You can't even spell *persnickety!"*

"Can too! I looked it up in the dictionary and when they used it in a sentence, they used *your name!"*

"Ha. Ha. That's so funny I forgot to laugh."

"Ever since you met that creep Cassandra you've become a different kid—"

"That's right—*a junior high kid!*"

I could see this argument was going nowhere. And it really hurt, because even though we were fighting, I still missed Paige as my friend. Especially at Halloween.

And sometimes I do things I know are impossible but I do them anyway because there's always the teeniest, tiniest chance that they might be possible. And if a girl doesn't try, she'll never find out for sure.

"Why don't you cancel your party and come to mine? It's Halloween, our favorite time of year. we can tell ghost stories, bob for apples, and have lots of fun—"

*"You wish!* Oh, and I forgot to tell you—I told my mom about the Smellys and she said if those juvenile delinquents start throwing eggs she's going to call the police! And if they run away before the police get there? We're going to tell the police to go to *your* party and arrest them! *And not only that*—they're going to arrest *you* for telling them to do it!"

"I didn't tell them to do anything! You made them mad by saying bad things about me! It's not my fault if they—"

"You can just tell that to the police!"

Then she hung up with a loud bang.

# 29

I didn't sleep well that night. I kept tossing and turning, wondering what had happened to Paige. I thought about all the years we were friends and how we almost never got in a fight. I thought about all the stuff we did together, the sleepovers when we slept outside under a full moon and listened to the *The Harley Sandwich Hour* on her portable radio. I thought about the dance we made up for those sleepovers. We called it the *moon dance,* and pretended like it was something magical. But all we really did was jerk our arms and legs around like Jerry Lewis getting electrocuted.

How could she not remember all the good stuff?

Then I thought about my party, and I worried about everything that could go wrong. Would Justin think it was a crappy party? Would Miriam wiggle her butt at Justin? Would the Smellys get me arrested?

And last of all, I worried about my costume—or lack of one—because it was starting to look like I'd be the only one at the party not wearing a costume.

Before I went to bed I asked mom to help me make a costume. But she just pulled out some of dad's greasy old work clothes and said I could go as a hobo. She'd been saving those clothes to use for cleaning rags, but now she was going to let me use them for a costume? Thanks, Miss Generous.

I told mom I didn't want to be a hobo, and asked if she could come up with something else. But all she did was grab some scarves and wrap them around dad's old clothes. And she called it a clown costume.

Being a hobo was bad enough, but a *hobo clown*? I mean, if I was going to sink that low, I might as well go as a hairy armpit.

I looked at Bonnie, who was fast asleep on the bed beside me and I thought how lucky she was to be a fifth grader and have no problems. Being a seventh-grader was really hard and it made me wish I was a little kid again. It was so easy then, the only thing I had to worry about was what flavor Popsicle I wanted from the Good Humor truck.

But, now I had giant problems.

Eventually I fell asleep but I had bad dreams all night.


I dreamed I was at my Halloween party and I kept putting food on the table, but every time I turned around, it was gone.

Everyone kept saying, "What kind of crappy party is this? Where's the food?" And I kept saying, "But I just put it down!" Then I looked up at the ceiling and saw the Smelly brothers on rubber cords. They dropped to the table like a couple of spiders, grabbed the food then bounced back to the ceiling. Before I could stop them, Miriam came in the door, and everyone turned to look at her.

Miriam was beautiful. She had a costume that was all sparkly like *Glenda the Good Witch* from the Wizard of Oz. And she was so pretty that Justin couldn't stop looking at her. And I tried to get Justin's attention, but when he turned to look at me, he just said, "What kind of costume is *that?*"

And I looked at myself and was shocked to see that I was wearing a costume that made me look like a goof. So I said, "I'm supposed to be Jerry Lewis."

Then Justin looked at me and said, "Is that pee on your pants?"

I looked down at my pants and was embarrassed to see a pee stain.

"Well, you see…I just got electrocuted…"

I woke up with a start.

The dream was so real I had to look under the covers to make sure I wasn't wearing a Jerry Lewis costume.

Thank goodness I was still in my pajamas.

And there was no pee stain.

# 30

I got very little sleep, so I was really dragging the next morning and it made me late getting to the bus stop. I wanted to get there early so I'd have time to talk to the Smellys, but I got there only a few minutes before the bus did.

"Melvin? Jacob? I need to talk to you." I nodded to the side, indicating that we should walk away from the other kids.

When they came over, they were still smiling with those dopey grins from yesterday.

"Yeah, Trudy?"

"Paige told me you guys are going to egg the kids at her party."

They both starting giggling. "We been stealing eggs from the refrigerator for weeks now," Melvin said.

"And we been storing them down by the furnace—" Jacob added.

"—so they'll be good and rotten—"

"—'cause rotten eggs stink the best!"

"I don't think that's such a good idea—"

"Don't worry, Trudy," Melvin wiped his nose on his sleeve. "We got lots of eggs. We'll still have plenty left for Halloween night—"

"Yeah, we'll only use a dozen on Paige's friends."

"That's still not a good idea. Paige's mom said she was going to call the police on you..."

Jacob giggled. "But we'll be in costumes—"

"—so Paige's mom won't know who did it!" Melvin laughed like a hyena and Jacob joined him.

"You don't understand." I had to raise my voice to be heard over the snorting. "The police will know who did it because you already told Paige your plans—"

"*You* don't understand," Melvin smirked. "Melvin and Jacob told Paige that they were going to egg her party, but Melvin and Jacob won't do it."

"Then, who will?"

"Huckleberry Hound and Casper the Friendly Ghost."

"But the police will still know—"

"The police would *never* suspect Huckleberry Hound and Casper the Friendly Ghost," Melvin insisted.

"That's right," Jacob added. "They might suspect Yogi Bear, or Woody Woodpecker, or Bugs Bunny—"

"But *not* Huckleberry Hound and Casper the Friendly Ghost."

Just then the bus pulled up and the Smellys ran to be the first ones on. "Don't worry, Trudy—" Jacob yelled over his shoulder as he shoved a kid out of the way.

"—we got it all figured out," Melvin added as he shoved Jacob out of the way.

As they got on the bus, I heard Melvin whisper to Jacob. *"Let's egg Paige's mom, too!"*

# 31

After I got home from school, I changed into my jeans and moped around the house.

As if I didn't have enough on my mind, now I had to worry about getting arrested at my own Halloween party. And worst of all? *I didn't even want the party!*

I could just see the police showing up at the basement door with Mrs. H. behind them, egg dripping off her face as she pointed to the Smellys. "That's them! Casper, and Huckleberry—they did it!" Then she'd point at me and say, "Arrest her too! She's the ringleader!"

Then they'd handcuff me with Justin watching, and he'd be all embarrassed and ashamed of me, and Miriam would hold his hand, and say, "I used to baby sit her. She's always been a rotten little brat..."

But the saddest thing of all? I wouldn't even have a Halloween costume.

The last great Halloween and I had no costume to get arrested in.

I'd done everything I could to get a bat costume but now my brain was all dried up. I had no more ideas, so I finally gave up. I stretched out on the sofa and just stared at the ceiling.

Nellie came around the corner in her fairy costume. She saw me and said, "I'm going to turn you into a frog!" Then she began bopping me on the head with her fairy wand. But I didn't care. I just kept staring at the ceiling.

When I didn't scream or hit her back, Nellie started crying. Then she ran to basement steps. "Mom! Mom! Trudy's *dead!*"

Mom came upstairs carrying a basket of laundry. "Who's dead?"

"Trudy! I hit her on the head with my wand and I killed her!" Nellie cried.

"Trudy! Stop scaring your little sister by pretending to be dead!"

"I didn't do anything. I was just lying here."

I guess I must have sounded pretty sad, because mom suddenly looked worried. "What's the matter?"

"Nothing."

"Don't *nothing* me! Now, what's the matter?"

I pulled myself up on one elbow. "It's nothing. I was just thinking that I don't have a Halloween costume and tomorrow is the party. That's all. No big deal. I just won't wear a costume—"

"Did you ask your Aunt Katie if she had one?"

*Huh?*

"Why would I ask her?"

"She used to have big Halloween parties every year."

"I don't remember Aunt Katie having parties."

"It was before you were born. Your dad and I used to go every year. Aunt Katie and her husband had the best Halloween parties in town."

"Why did she stop?"

"I guess she lost interest when her husband died."

"Did she ever dress up?"

"Oh my yes! Aunt Katie and her husband wore the most creative costumes you ever saw! She would start working on them in August and by Halloween they were so elaborate you'd swear she got them right off a movie screen."

I jumped off the sofa and threw on my sweatshirt. "Why didn't you tell me this before?"

"I guess I never thought—"

I was out the door and halfway up the hill when mom yelled, "While you're there—see if she has party favors!"

# 32

Aunt Katie! Why didn't I think of her before?

Maybe I didn't know about her Halloween parties, but I should have remembered that Aunt Katie has the best ideas in the world. And Aunt Katie isn't like other adults, she doesn't talk down to me, or tell me I should *grow up* or anything like that. And while Aunt Katie may be an old lady, she still has the brain of a kid.

I was so happy I was practically skipping down the road. I just knew Aunt Katie would have something I could use for a costume. *I just knew it!*

I never got to know Aunt Katie's husband because he died when I was a baby, but before he died he was a merchant marine and brought Aunt Katie neat stuff from all over the world. I could just imagine the kind of Halloween treasures she had lurking in her attic!

To get to Aunt Katie's I had to pass Paige's house, and I was hoping she'd be outside. If Paige was there I was going to smile and wave and pretend like we were still friends. Because sometimes when you pretend hard enough, it comes true.

But as I got to the edge of Paige's property, a car pulled over and a girl got out carrying an overnight bag. As I got closer I saw it was that creep Cassandra.

It was too late for me to cross the road to avoid her, so I just walked straight ahead, hoping she wouldn't see me.

But she did.

*"Trudy!"* She waved, and walked over to me as the car pulled away. "My mom just dropped me off. I'm going to spend the night at Paige's house so we can get ready for the party tomorrow."

I knew she was trying to rub it in, so I pretended like I didn't care. "That's nice," I said in snotty way.

"Planning a party is such a big job. Paige and I even have to go shopping before the party tomorrow."

Cassandra must have got Paige to wring more money out of her mother.

But why should I care?

"That's nice," I said in the same snotty voice. "But I have to do some party planning of my own, so if you'll get out of my way—"

"What was the name of the boy you were going to bring to Paige's party?"

I was really tired of Cassandra trying to rub things in my face. "Why do you care?"

"I don't really," she said with smile. "But Miriam told me a boy is taking her to your party."

So, ol' Miriam got some boy to take her to my party? Well, good for her.

"So what? Miriam can bring anyone she wants—"

"I just wondered because she said he goes to Loyola High School…"

It couldn't be.

It must be a coincidence.

"…and I remembered that you were going to bring a Loyola boy to Paige's party, so I wondered if the boys knew each other."

"It's possible. Justin might—"

"That's him!" she said with a happy smirk. "Miriam said her date's name is Justin!"

# 33

All the spit dried up in my mouth. I didn't even have enough saliva to speak, so I just walked away from Cassandra without saying a word.

I heard her giggle behind my back, and wished there was snow on the ground so I could pelt her with a snowball. A big icy one with a rock in it.

My legs kept walking to Aunt Katie's house but my mind wasn't part of the trip. I was brain-numb. I knew Justin wasn't my date or anything, he was just a friend—but how could he do it? How could he bring another girl to my party? And just thinking about it made me queasy, like I'd just eaten a whole stick of butter.

As I stumbled along, I thought about Miriam and the more I thought about her, the madder I got. *I* invited Justin to my party—*not Miriam!* What right did she have to take him over? And how did that happen? Did she ask him to take her?

*I bet she did!*

Miriam's real grabby like that, and Justin's such a nice guy that he probably didn't want to hurt her feelings, so he said *yes!*

Or—did Justin ask her?

Maybe he thought about her lying in the grass this summer, staring at him and wiggling her rear end. Maybe he heard she was coming and called her on the phone and asked her to be his date.

Just thinking about it made my stomach hurt even more.

But who told Justin that Miriam was coming to my party?

Only one answer—*the Smellys!*

Those rotten boys walk past Justin's house every day as they come and go to the bus stop. They must have seen Justin washing his dad's car in the driveway, and told him!

I could just image it.


*"Hey Justin! Are you going to Trudy's party?"*

*"Yes, I am."*

*"Do you have a date? Because it will look weird if a high school boy does not bring a date."*

*"Oh. I did not think of that. Thanks for telling me boys. Do you think I should ask Trudy to be my date?"*

*"No! You don't want to ask Trudy! She's only eleven years old!"*

*"But then, who?"*

*"You should ask Miriam because she's thirteen, and she'll be fourteen in February."*

*"Do you think she will go with me?"*

*"Of course! Why do you think she rolls on her stomach and wiggles her behind whenever she sees you?"*

*"Oh. I did not think of that. I guess that means she likes me. Thanks for pointing that out fellas."*

*"No problem! Here's Miriam's phone number—"*

I didn't know if it happened like that or not, all I knew was that Justin and Miriam were now coming as a couple. And I didn't think I could stand seeing them together. Just imagining them standing close to each other or holding hands made me feel like crying. And I sure-as-shootin' didn't want to cry in front of them.

But I couldn't un-invite them either.

Because if I did that, I'd have to tell them why and I didn't want them to know how upset I was. It would have just *killed me* if Miriam knew I was hurt. And it would have been even worse if Justin knew, 'cause then he'd know how much I like him. And if he knew how bad I felt, he would pity me. *Poor little seventh-grader likes a high school boy, don't you feel sorry for her?*

I couldn't stand seeing them together, but I couldn't avoid it either.

So, what could I do?

# 34

I was sorry now that I hadn't listened to my mother when she said I was too old for Halloween. If I'd have listened to her I wouldn't have wasted so much time trying to make a bat costume. And I wouldn't have planned a party with Paige, or invited Justin. Then they'd both still be my friends.

The sun was going down and it was starting to get dark. October is like that, it gets dark early. I used to think that was spooky-neat, but today it just felt cold. As I walked along, I shuffled through piles of dried leaves. I used to have fun kicking leaves into the air, but now I didn't even try. I guess mom was right. I guess I was too old for this Halloween stuff.

I had originally imagined my costume as silky black with sequins to make it look like moonlight bouncing off the wings. But what difference did it make now? Paige wasn't going to be at the party so she couldn't see how cool it was. Justin would be with Miriam so he probably wouldn't even notice me. So, why should I wear a costume at all?

I suddenly felt stupid for wanting a costume.

Mom was right, Halloween costumes were for little kids.

I didn't want a costume anymore, so I didn't need to go to Aunt Katie's house.

I was going to turn around and go home, but I'd have to walk by Paige's house, and if I saw her in the yard with Cassandra I might start crying. I couldn't stand the idea of Cassandra seeing me cry, so I just kept going. It would be dark in another hour, then I could go home without anyone seeing me.

I got to Aunt Katie's house and knocked. It usually takes Aunt Katie a long time to get to the door because she has the arthritis really bad and she walks real slow. But I only knocked once and she surprised me by opening the door right away.

"Well, it's about time!" she said with a smile. "You're mom called twenty minutes ago and said you were on your way. I was starting to get worried!"

There was something about Aunt Katie that looked different. I noticed she wasn't wearing her glasses, so that was one thing, but there was something else. She was standing up straight, not leaning from of the pain in her bones, but it was more than that. It made me think of the

Frankenstein movie when Dr. Frankenstein throws the switch and the monster comes alive. There was something *electric* about Aunt Katie.

"Well, don't just stand there, Trudy—come on in!"

I walked in and saw a bunch of picture books lying on the davenport.

"Your mom said, you're having a Halloween party, so I got out the old photo albums of my parties to give you some ideas. Sit down—let me show you what I've got!" Aunt Katie got to the sofa faster than I'd ever seen her move before.

"Is your arthritis gone?"

"What? Oh, no, it still hurts. But I'm ignoring it today. Come on, sit down!"

She was so happy and excited, I didn't know how to tell her I wasn't interested in Halloween, so I just sat down. Aunt Katie immediately plopped a picture album in my lap and began flipping through the pages. She stopped when she came to a picture of two people in Halloween costumes. "Can you guess who these two are?"

It was a picture of some guy dressed as Popeye the Sailor and standing next to him was a young woman dressed like an old-time airplane pilot with seaweed around her neck. "Uh, no...."

Aunt Katie's laughter sounded like wind chimes. "That's me and my husband, Henry!"

I looked again and could finally see the resemblance between the young woman in the picture and my Aunt Katie.

"That's so neat! Your husband is Popeye. But who are you supposed to be?"

"I was Amelia Earhart. She disappeared about eight years before, so I dressed up as Amelia with seaweed around my neck. I told everyone Popeye pulled me out of the water and kept me on his ship for eight years. Some people thought my costume was in bad taste, but I didn't care. It was Halloween and anyone who couldn't join in the fun was free to leave the party."

"That's so cool!" I could just see my Aunt Katie telling some jerk to get lost. It made me wish Cassandra was coming to my party just so I could throw her out.

She flipped a few pages and pointed to another picture. "Do you know who these two are?"

It was a picture of a woman dressed like a big pumpkin and a man wearing a hillbilly costume. They looked a lot younger, but I still recognized them. "That's my mom and dad!"

"That's right! Your mom was pregnant with you at the time, that's why she was such a big pumpkin, and your dad was Lil' Abner from the funny pages."

"I never knew they wore Halloween costumes…"

"We all used to dress up. I had a big party every year, and—wait a minute—let me show you another picture…" She flipped through the albums until she found the one she was looking for.

"There! Guess who they are."

It was a picture of a man dressed as an angel and a woman in a devil's costume. The devil had zigzag wings and horns and she aimed a pitchfork at the angel. The angel acted like he didn't care, he just held his arms behind his back, like he was trying to straighten his posture. Although he was younger and had a full head of dark hair, I only know one person who does that posture thing…

"That's grandpa!" I yelled. "But who's that woman in the devil costume?"

"That's your grandmother."

"*Grandma?* But she just gave me a big lecture because I wanted to be a bat for Halloween! She called it a devil creature and said I shouldn't want to be a creature of the night. And there she is in a devil costume…"

"That was a long time ago. Your grandma was between religions at the time so she had no limitations." Aunt Katie put her glasses on and looked at the picture. "And that's why my husband and I had our Halloween parties. It gave our friends the opportunity to be kids again."

I thought of all the times I got bossed around, told what to eat, when to go to bed and when to get up. "Why would an adult want to give up their freedom to be a kid?"

*"Freedom?"* Aunt Katie snorted like I'd just said something funny. "Let me put it to you this way—when I was a kid I used to pretend I was Tom Swift. He was a character in a book who invented all kinds of amazing things. I'd go to the dump and collect all kinds of junk for my inventions. I spent many days happily creating spaceships and submarines and getting the other kids to pretend my inventions were real. So, what do you think would happen to me if I did that now?"

I thought about Aunt Katie digging junk out of trashcans for pretend inventions and what her nosey neighbors would say.

"I guess if you did that now they'd lock you up in a looney bin."

"So, *who* has more freedom?"

# 35

Aunt Katie flipped through the photo albums, showing me all the different costumes. "Look at them," she said, smiling. "Look how happy everyone is! It's important to always stay a child in your heart. And that's what Halloween's about— letting the child come out. Halloween helps us remember that we have—"

"Potential," I said, voicing my secret thought.

"Maybe…but I was going to say—*no limits.* As we grow older we give ourselves too many limits. Like your grandma saying bats are evil, or—"

"—or neighbors thinking an old lady is crazy for digging in trashcans."

Aunt Katie snorted and nodded. "True, true. I guess I always liked Halloween because we have no limits. Your dad believed he could be someone from the funny pages, your grandma believed she could be a devil, and I believed I could be a famous pilot—"

"But sometimes it hurts to believe."

I didn't want to talk about the stuff that was bugging me but it popped out of my mouth anyway.

Aunt Katie peered at me over her glasses. "What's that supposed to mean?"

"I mean, sometimes you believe something…" I thought about Justin and how I believed he liked me, and I thought of Paige and how I believed she was my best friend. "…but then you find out it isn't true and it hurts."

"Well, that's the trouble with believing. Sometimes you believe something is true and when it doesn't turn out the way you expected, you believe it *isn't* true. Either way you're giving yourself limits."

I couldn't' wrap my brain around what she was saying. I must have had a dumb look on my face because Aunt Katie turned to another page in the album.

"Look here," she pointed to a picture of a woman with long blonde hair wearing a white satin evening gown and holding a long cigarette holder.

"Wow, she's really pretty."

"Veronica was extremely beautiful. I used to be so jealous of her. Before we got married, my Henry went steady with her and everyone was sure he was going to marry her. I was crazy about Henry but Veronica was so beautiful I didn't think I'd ever have a chance with him."

"What'd you do?"

153

"I stopped believing." Aunt Katie bent forward and stared at the picture of the pretty girl. "I stopped believing I didn't have a chance. I stopped believing Henry was going to marry Veronica and I stopped believing she was more beautiful than me."

"So, you started believing you were going to marry him?"

"No. I just stopped believing that I wouldn't."

"That's kind of backwards."

"Oh yeah? Well, look at this—" she pulled three old pictures from the album and laid them on the coffee table next to each other.

I never knew my Uncle Henry, but he was really handsome. In the picture he was wearing some kind of uniform, he had a great smile, and the kind of chin only movie stars have. The pretty girl also looked like a movie star with long blonde hair, straight teeth and dimples in her cheeks. But my Aunt Katie had a crooked smile, her nose had a bend in it, and her hair was kind of wild.

"So, who do you think that handsome guy married?"

"The dopey looking girl?"

Aunt Katie laughed so hard she had to slap her knee to get it all out. "That's right! He married the dopey looking girl with the backwards thinking!"

I hadn't seen my Aunt Katie that happy in a long time. Just watching her laugh made me feel good.

"All right! Enough of this old stuff! Let's get you a Halloween costume. You said you wanted to be a bat for Halloween?"

"Yeah, but…"

"I've still got that old devil costume of your grandma's. The wings look about right, and if I cut the horns down, I could make them look like bat ears—"

I didn't want a costume anymore. I didn't want to dress up because I had no one to impress—but my Aunt Katie looked so excited and happy when she talked about making costumes. So, I thought—who cares?

Who cares about Justin, who cares about Paige, who cares about Miriam or Cassandra?

*This is my Halloween!*

I looked at the devil costume in the picture. The whole costume was perfect, the wings, the hood, even the legs and arms. Everything was perfect. Except for one thing. "But…Aunt Katie, that costume is red."

"So? You don't believe bats can be red?"

"Well… I don't believe they *can't* be."

# 36

It took a long time to find that old costume and when we did Aunt Katie had to cut and sew the horns to make them look like ears. She also had to shorten the legs and arms so I didn't trip all over myself. And while we were in the attic she also found a big box of Halloween stuff; noise makers, clickety-clack spinners, papier-mâché pumpkins, and a witch game that told your fortune. And she gave it all to me.

Aunt Katie called my mom and said I was going to have dinner with her and she'd bring me home later. Then we had hot dogs, popcorn and cake for dinner, which is now officially my favorite meal.

It was almost 8:00 o'clock by the time we finished. Aunt Katie doesn't like to drive because her eyes are bad, but she said I could be her eyes while we drove to my house. She can see the road okay, but it was my job to make sure we didn't run over a cat or anything. On the way home, I was so busy being Aunt Katie's eyes that I didn't even notice when we passed Paige's house.

I got up early the next day because I had a lot to do for the party. I took the stuff Aunt Katie gave me and put it on the table and it made everything look super Halloweeny.

Mom made candy apples and fudge the night before, and when she put them on the Halloween table it looked like a buffet at the Taj Mahal. Then mom helped me set up the bobbing-for-apples game, and she pushed pennies into the apples for prizes. She even put a dime in a couple of them. "Make sure you tell everyone there's money in these apples," she warned. "I don't want some kid swallowing a coin." And I promised her I would make sure everyone knew.

Even my father helped with the party.

Dad left grandpa in charge of the garage so he could come to the house and carve a bunch of jack-o-lanterns. I figured dad was having a good time carving pumpkins because a couple times I caught him chuckling like a little kid. And when we finally got to see his creations, we discovered what he was laughing about. He gave all the pumpkins crazy faces, two had empty beers bottles stuck in their mouths, and a couple of them were smoking cigarettes.

And when mom saw those pumpkins and just said, "Oh, Dale…" and that made dad laugh even harder.

After dad went back to the garage, mom took the cigarettes and beer bottles out of the pumpkins. When I caught her doing it, she said, "It might give Jacob and Melvin ideas." And I had to agree.

I was so busy setting things up for the party I didn't even have a chance to think about Justin or Paige. But while I was outside raking a big pile of leaves for the little kids to jump in, I noticed someone walking down the hill. It took a minute, but I finally realized it was Paige.

Oh, no.

The Smellys jumped the gun and started egging kids early. A fine pair of criminals those two are. They didn't even wait until it got dark so no one would see them.

I figured Paige was going to yell at me, so I walked halfway up the hill to meet her. Everyone at my house was having such a good time getting ready for the party I didn't want them to hear yelling.

When I got to Paige, I said, "Okay, what did the Smellys do?"

But instead of answering, she just broke down crying.

# 37

*Did the Smellys egg her mother to death?*

"Paige, why are you crying? What's the matter?"

She tried to talk between sobs. "A brat...you were right...my fault...and crazy..."

"Stop! Stop! I don't know what you're trying to say! Sit down until you stop crying."

Paige nodded, sat on the ground and began taking deep breaths. I sat next to her and waited. When she finally stopped crying, I asked, "Okay, what's the matter?"

"Cassandra. You were right about her. We went shopping this morning for stuff for the party. She said she had plenty of money, but she didn't."

"She made you pay for everything?"

"Worse. She started stuffing things in a bag without paying for them."

*"Shoplifting?"*

"Yeah. And she made fun of me because I wouldn't do it."

"Did you help her?"

"No, but that didn't stop her. She just kept stuffing more stuff into the bag. Then suddenly she pushed me into the lady's room, handed me the bag and ran into one of the stalls. I thought she just wanted me to hold it while she went to the toilet, but then a saleslady came in and asked to see a receipt for the stuff in the bag."

"Oh, no..."

"Oh, yes. And I told the saleslady the bag belonged to my friend. But when Cassandra came out off the stall she told the saleslady it wasn't her bag."

"She lied on you?"

"She sure did. Then the saleslady took us to the office and they called my mom to come pick us up. And Cassandra kept telling everyone that she didn't do it, that it was me who stole all that stuff."

"What a creep!"

"I know right? When mom picked us up I started yelling at Cassandra to tell the truth, but mom was so angry she told me to just *shut up,* and she put Cassandra in the backseat and me in the front seat. But on the way home I got so mad I jumped over the seat and started wailing on Cassandra. I just kept hitting her and telling her to tell the truth. My mom couldn't do anything because she was driving, so she was yelling and I was yelling and Cassandra was yelling. *But I couldn't stop!* I was so mad I told Cassandra if she didn't tell the truth I was going to pull all her hair out until she was bald. And to prove it, I pulled a out a big chunk—"

"Gosh Paige!"

"I know! I just went crazy!"

"Did she ever tell the truth?"

"When she saw my hand full of her precious hair, she finally confessed."

"What happened?"

"As soon as we got home, mom told Cassandra to get her overnight bag because she was going to drive her home. Then mom told me to call everyone and tell them my party was cancelled."

"Oh, man…"

"So when I called all the kids I told them why the party was cancelled and how Cassandra lied on me. And you know what they said?"

"What?"

"They said Cassandra was a big jerk, and they didn't know why I was friends with her in the first place. They said the only reason they were coming to my party was because they liked *me,* not *her!*"

"Holy maroly!"

"And you want to know something else? When my mom got back from taking Cassandra home she asked why I wasn't still friends with you, because you're a much better influence than Cassandra."

"Your mom said I was a good influence?"

"Yeah. How 'bout that?"

All these years Mrs. H. didn't like me because she thought I was the one who got Paige in trouble. Now she thinks I'm the good one? That *really* made me happy!

"I was crazy to listen to all that crap Cassandra told me. And I'm sorry for everything I said and did. I'll understand if you don't want to be my friend anymore."

Not want to be friends anymore? Was she kidding?

"Not only do I want you to be my friend, but I'd really like it if you'd help me with my Halloween party. I'm going to need someone to help run the contests and tell ghost stories, and—"

"And all the stuff we planned."

"Right. All the stuff we planned ever since we were little kids."

"Thanks Trudy." Paige got kind of teary. "I really need to feel like a little kid, again."

"I guess after all that stuff Cassandra was planning for your party; dance contests—"

"—spin the bottle, bite the apple, seven minutes in heaven —"

"What's that?"

"You don't even wanna' know. I'm just glad I don't have to do it." Paige suddenly got real happy. "*I know!* I'll go home and get all the Halloween decorations and the contest prizes we picked out—"

"The good prizes, not that junk Cassandra wanted."

"Don't worry. The junk she wanted was the stuff she was shoplifting. You don't have to worry about that crap coming to our party."

"That's right, *our* party."

Paige smiled so big her face looked like it was going to split in two.

"Yeah. *Our* party."

# 38

Paige went home to get the Halloween stuff. But before she left, I asked mom if Paige could stay for dinner and she said that would be fine. I told Paige when she came back to bring her Halloween costume and she could get dressed for the party after dinner.

I was glad Paige was going to help me for a lot of reason. First off, I really needed the help. There were going to be fifteen kids at the party and that was a lot of kids to keep under control. And when you counted the Smelly brothers that was like having thirty kids.

But also, Paige would be there when Justin got to the party. She was my best friend so I wouldn't feel alone. And with her there, I'd be distracted from watching Justin and Miriam.

After dinner we all got into our costumes. Bonnie, Danny and Nellie were finally allowed into the basement and they oohed and ahhed at all the decorations. And I had to admit, it was spectacular. With Paige's decorations, the stuff I bought, the jack-o-lanterns dad made, mom's food, and all of Aunt

Katie's stuff it looked like the kind of Halloween party you see in *The Post* magazine.

Everything was in place, the tub with the apples for bobbing, the spin-the-wheel witch fortune teller, the bean bag toss, and all the food was on the table.

"Wow, Trudy," Paige said. "Your bat costume is so cool!"

"I know, right?"

I was really happy with the costume. It was red satin that shimmered and shined. And the wings were perfect; they had a zigzag cut that made them look wicked and they were attached to the arms so I could open and close them like a real bat. Mom put some red lipstick on me, and she used her eyebrow pencil to draw bat whiskers on my face. I had some plastic fangs, but they didn't fit in my mouth, so I just chucked them. The whole costume was way cooler than anything I ever imagined.

Everything was perfect.

Except for one thing.

Justin would be with someone else.

I forced myself to stop thinking about Justin and Miriam. "Your costume is really neat, too, Paige."

"Yeah, I guess, but I think it's a little too girly. I mean, I like the sparkly wings, but I don't like wearing a dress that has no straps to hold up the top."

"But that's what Tinkerbell's dress looks like."

"I know, but it makes me worry. It's the kind of thing the Smellys like to grab and pull down."

"True. But I'll watch out for you."

The party was supposed to start at 6:00, but since it got dark then, some of the little kids came earlier.

Nellie was beside herself with joy when one of the kids showed up in a Howdy Doody costume—her great love. She ran around him, bonking him on the head with her fairy wand to put a love spell on him. I made her stop before Howdy started crying.

Bonnie looked real pretty in her 1800's girl costume. Her friend Anna came to the party dressed as Dale Evans, and she pulled out her shiny, rapid-fire cap pistols for Bonnie to admire. In response, Bonnie waved her wrist under Anna's nose so she could admire the rhinestone bracelet mom let her wear. Then Anna aimed her gun at Bonnie and tried to rob her. Who knew Dale Evans was such a scoundrel?

Danny wore his hobo costume and mom used her eyebrow pencil to draw a beard on his chin. Danny squashed an empty toilet paper roll and wrapped electrical tape around it to make it look like a cigar. His friend Leroy showed up in a similar hobo costume and liked Danny's cigar so much, they went upstairs to liberate a roll of toilet paper from its tube. Mom was gonna' love that.

I tried not to think about Justin and Miriam, but as it got closer to 6:00, I kept going outside and looking up the driveway. It was dark by then, and dad put the porch light on so everyone could find their way down the hill. At 6:15 I finally saw Justin and Miriam coming down the driveway.

Justin looked so cool. He was wearing a black suit with a vest and a red sash across his chest. He wore a big cape over the whole thing, so he really looked like Dracula—that is—if vampires wore glasses and had buckteeth instead of fangs.

But just looking at him made my heart hurt.

It was cold out so Miriam was wearing a coat, but under it she wore a puffy dress with lots of petticoats. She was also wearing her hair in an upsweep hairdo with a rhinestone tiara. Although there wasn't much light from the porch, I could tell her older sister had put lots of makeup on her, so she looked like a real queen. I'd never see Miriam look so pretty. No wonder Justin wanted to be her date.

I looked down at my bat costume and wondered why I ever wanted to be a bat in the first place. My costume seemed so dorky now. And I wished I'd chosen something more grown-up. Just watching Justin and Miriam together made me realize what a perfect couple they were. They would probably go steady, get married, and...

Then I remembered three photographs; a beautiful girl, a handsome boy, and a dorky girl with wiry hair and a crooked smile.

And it was really weird because as soon as I thought of those pictures, it was like I was looking at everything through a View-Master stereoscopic viewer. When I thought of Aunt Katie's pictures, it was like I pushed the lever and the picture changed. Suddenly Miriam and Justin weren't boyfriend and girlfriend anymore, just two kids coming down the driveway. And I wasn't a dorky kid anymore—I was just a girl in a bat costume.

And a really cool costume, at that.

"Oh, man, look at that Miriam," Paige said, coming up next to me on the stoop. "Why would she wear high-heel shoes when she knew she'd have to come down your driveway?"

Miriam was having a hard time making it down the driveway. She kept stumbling on the gravel, and every time she tripped, Justin would grab her arm and help her stand up.

"Maybe she just wanted her date to hold her arm." I was really proud of myself because I said it without wanting to cry.

"Date? He isn't Miriam's date."

"But he's bringing her to my party."

"Yeah, he's bringing her—but not as a date! Justin has to walk by her house to get here, so Miriam asked him to bring her."

"Isn't that a date?"

"Heck no! She only asked him to bring her because she's afraid of the dark!"

*Of course!*

I knew Miriam was afraid of the dark! After the baseball games we'd all sit around and look at the stars, but Miriam always had someone walk her home. She's been afraid of the dark as long as I've known her.

"What made you think he was her date?"

"Cassandra. She told me Justin was Miriam's date."

"Miriam bragged to Cassandra that a boy was bringing her to your party. But when I asked Miriam about it, she told me the truth." Paige put her arms around her bare shoulders and shivered. "I'll see you downstairs. I'm cold." She went back in the house just as Justin and Miriam walked up to the stoop.

"Hey Trudy," Justin said with a smile. "I almost didn't recognize you in your costume. That's really cool."

"You look really cool, too." I felt my cheeks get hot and a stupid grin spread across my face. "And you look real pretty, Miriam." I didn't even have to fake it. I said it with complete sincerity.

"So, what're you supposed to be?" Miriam asked, adjusting her crooked tiara.

"A bat."

"There's no such thing as a red bat."

"Maybe there never used to be," I said as I spread my glorious satin wings. "But there is now."

# 39

It was the best Halloween party ever.

Paige helped with all the games and everyone had a good time. The Smellys bobbed for Apples and when Melvin got the apple with the dime in it, Jacob got mad and tried to bite every apple in the tub to find another one. But Justin told him to knock it off. A little while later I saw Jacob slip the dime out of his brother's pocket.

The only other trouble the Smellys got into was when Melvin said, "Want to see me make a pumpkin pie?" Then he jumped on one of the Jack-o-lanterns and smashed it. Justin got really mad and made them clean it up. Then he said, "You guys are guests here. Act like gentlemen." And for some reason that made the Smellys behave. I guess no one ever called them a gentleman before.

Miriam was the oldest girl at the party but it didn't seem to bother her. She played with everyone and looked like she was having a good time. It didn't even bother me when Justin talked to her. I was actually glad he paid attention to her, 'cause she looked kinda' weird hanging around with just the little kids.

It finally got to be time for the ghost story. Paige rounded everyone up and made them sit in a semi-circle around me then she turned off all the lights. I sat near the furnace so the spooky light from the flames would flicker across my face.

I told the story about a strange man I met on the road near a campfire. He was very thin and I started asking him questions about why his feet were so thin and he said, *up late and little eat.* And I kept asking questions about his legs and knees and all the way up to his neck and the answer was always the same, *up late and little eat.* And every time I said it, I used a soft, whispery voice. Then, when I asked him why his mouth was so thin, Paige yelled, *"So I can eat you!"* And everybody screamed.

It was really cool, except Nelly got scared and started crying. Then she ran upstairs to tell mom, but mom just said, "You're supposed to get scared on Halloween. Stop acting

172

like a baby." That was the first time mom ever took my side against Nellie.

After an hour, mom came downstairs with a tray of popcorn balls and everyone grabbed one.

"Wow, mom, did you just make these?"

"No, your Aunt Katie did."

"*Aunt Katie's here!* Tell her to join the party!"

"She can't. It hurts her hips to go up and down these stairs."

So Paige and I gathered everyone together and said we were going to have a costume parade. We told everyone we were going to march around my mom, dad and Aunt Katie and they were going to pick the best costumes.

So, everyone lined up and we marched upstairs and paraded around the adults. And the three of them clapped their hands and oohed and ahhed, and acted scared by the costumes. My Aunt Katie and my parents were laughing and hugging each other as the parade went around them and I think they had as much fun as the kids. Justin was at the end of the line and when he got to my Aunt Katie he took her hand and pretended like he was going to bite it but she just laughed and swatted him away. Then we all marched downstairs while the judges made up their minds.

Miriam got the prize for the prettiest costume, and a couple other kids got prizes for scariest and funniest, and even Jacob got a prize for being the friendliest because he was Casper the Friendly Ghost. I thought Melvin would get mad, but he didn't. I guess Melvin was just happy that one of them got to win something. And Jacob was so happy he gave Melvin back the dime he lifted.

The party was over at 8:30 so mom came downstairs and told everyone my dad was going to walk them up the hill to make sure they got home okay. Everyone moaned 'cause we were having so much fun no one wanted to leave.

Since my dad offered to walk Miriam home, I thought Justin would hang around for a while. I was so busy with the party I didn't get much chance to talk to him. But Justin just said, "Okay, queenie, are you ready to go?" And Miriam said yes, and they walked to the door. Then Justin told me it was the best Halloween party he'd ever been to, and he thanked me for inviting him.

And I stood at the door waving until the stumbling queen and the bucktooth vampire disappeared into the night.

# 40

**Gilbert Chemistry Set Experiment Book**

**Date:** *Monday, October 31, 1960*

**Experiment Objective:** *See what it's like to go out on Halloween without a costume.*

**Steps:**

**1.** *Told mom I would take the kids out trick-or-treating. She said she didn't think I would watch out for them, but I told her I wasn't going to wear a costume or go trick-or-treating myself so I would take good care of the kids. She fainted. (Just kidding.)*

**2.** *Told my brother and sisters they'd have to give me a cut of their Halloween candy since I wasn't trick-or-treating. They complained, but I told them I knew where all the good houses were and they'd get a better haul with me than with mom. That shut them up.*

175

**3.** *Got dad's big flashlight, put on my jeans and tennis shoes for lots of walking. Also hid a rubber monster mask in my pocket to scare my sisters and brother on the way home. After all, it's Halloween.*

**Result:** *Just experimenting. Not sure if I will like this or not.*

It got dark early so it was really spooky as we walked around the neighborhood trick-or-treating. True to my word, I skipped all the cheap houses that only gave you one crummy circus peanut, or a lousy apple, and I took the kids to the houses where I knew they gave out chocolate bars and loads of good candy. Passing on all of my trick-or-treat knowledge that I'd collected over the years was like giving my brother and sisters a Halloween inheritance.

It was a great night, cold, but with clear skies so we could see a million stars. It made me wish I could see the silhouette of a witch riding her broom through the night. That would be so cool.

Every once in a while the wind blew and dried leaves went skittering past us. I told the kids those were the ghosts of children who never got treats and they were coming to haunt the people who didn't give out Halloween candy. Then I made Danny, Bonnie and Nellie swear they'd always honor Halloween and when they grew up they'd always give good candy to the trick-or-treaters. They each made a solemn vow, crossed their hearts and hoped to die if they didn't.

As I walked along, I looked at all the kids in costumes, searching for Paige. Normally we'd go trick-or-treating together, but not this year. I told Paige she could come with me and the kids, but she decided to join the Smellys and egg the cheap people's houses. I think Paige knocked some brains loose when she got in that fight with Cassandra.

I didn't see Miriam and I wondered where she was tonight. Was she out clunking around the neighborhood in her high-heel shoes? She's scared of the dark, so if she were out trick-or-treating she'd be with a big group of kids.

Or with Justin.

I really wasn't sure about those two.


Eventually we got to the Pineleigh development. All the houses are new and we usually get lots of candy. There are no old ladies in the development, either. Old ladies are kinda' funny, they either give you really good stuff (like Aunt Katie) or they give you sticky old hard candy left over from when Moses parted the Red Sea.

As we got to the street where Justin lived, I considered skipping his house. Not because his family gives cheap candy or anything, but because I felt kind of weird about going up to his door. 'Cause if he was out with Miriam, I really didn't want to know.

But since Danny knew where Justin lived, I didn't want to make up a story about why we were skipping his house. Instead, I just let the kids go to the door while I stayed in the shadows.

*"Trick or treat!"* they yelled when the door opened.

My heart jumped when I saw Justin handing out the candy.

*"Hey!"* he said, dropping candy into their bags. "I know you guys! You're the McFarlan kids! Where's Trudy tonight?"

"She's over there." Nellie pointed at me while simultaneously unwrapping the candy Justin gave her.

I walked out of the shadows and waved.

"Hey Trudy! What are you doing?"

"Oh, just taking the kids trick-or-treating."

"Yeah? Sounds like fun."

Justin just kind of stood in the door and looked at me and I didn't really know what to do. The kids got their candy and ran from his house back to the sidewalk, so I had to go. I turned my back and started walking away. But...

...sometimes I do things I know are impossible but I do them anyway because there's always the teeniest, tiniest chance that they might be possible. And if a girl doesn't try, she'll never find out for sure.

I turned back to Justin. "Would you like to come with us?"

"Sure. Let me get my jacket."

The kids were already at the next house by the time Justin got his jacket, so we hurried to catch them. And while we were walking, the strangest thing happened.

Justin reached out and took my hand.

And I was glad it was dark because that stupid grin came back and took over my whole face.

*The End*

Proof

43266636R00105